PUNTERS

PUNTERS

Herbert Williams

GOMER

First Impression—2002

ISBN 1 84323 116 6

This book is published with the support of the
Arts Council of Wales.

Printed in Wales at
Gomer Press, Llandysul, Ceredigion

For my wife

ALSO BY HERBERT WILLIAMS:

FICTION
A Severe Case of Dandruff
The Woman in Back Row
The Stars in Their Courses
Stories of King Arthur

POETRY
Too Wet for the Devil
The Dinosaurs
A Lethal Kind of Love
The Trophy
Ghost Country
Looking Through Time

BIOGRAPHY
Davies the Ocean: Railway King and Coal Tycoon
John Cowper Powys

OTHER NON-FICTION
Come Out Wherever You Are
Railways in Wales
Stage Coaches in Wales
Battles in Wales
Voices of Wales
The Pembrokeshire Coast National Park

AUTHOR'S NOTE

This novel is set in a fictionalised Cardiff in the late 1990s. I have taken the liberty of advancing the arrival of the National Assembly for Wales by a few years. The suburb of Hollybush does not exist. All the characters are imaginary.

1

What she most despised about her husband was his virtue. She could put up with his politics, his pipe, even his occasional halitosis, but his unremitting goodness she abhorred. His toleration of her impossible behaviour was a kind of provocation. She felt, at times, tried beyond endurance.

'You're mad,' said Joyce, who lived next door. 'You don't deserve a man like that.'

'I know,' she cried passionately. 'I know I *know*. That's what makes it so utterly incredibly awful.'

And Joyce would go away thinking she just liked being theatrical.

It was true in a way: she did. But at the same time she meant it. Colin *did* infuriate her. There were times when she regretted marrying him, but usually she regretted nothing at all. There was a strange kind of fatalism about it. They had to meet; she had to marry him.

He knew her feelings, but never let on. He had made up his mind that theirs would be a perfect marriage, and nothing he said or did would invalidate that. When she sat there seething he would smile at her, the very image of contentment. The soft put-put of his lips on the stem of the pipe, the curl of the smoke, his benign expression, would irritate her so much that she felt she must scream or explode. But she too had her pride and her emotions found release in the violence of their lovemaking. She would take him in a fury with the very idea of him. And he would respond gratefully, matching his wilfulness to hers until they reached heights of pleasure that left them fulfilled and exhausted. She was grateful to him then, her legs entwined with his as they gave themselves to sleep. They were, in a way, a perfectly balanced couple.

They lived in Hollybush, a smart suburb on the very edge of Cardiff. Every morning he drove his company car smoothly from the garage along the new roads that led to Cardiff Bay, while she stayed at home. She told everyone she was between jobs, but secretly she did not want to work again, ever. She had suffered a breakdown after the death of her father and had lost faith in herself. They had only been crap jobs anyway; she wasn't qualified for anything much. She occupied herself in an old-fashioned way, treating the house as something to be nurtured, like a plant or a child. She was proud of it without being fussily house-proud. Small jars of herbs stood on a shelf in the kitchen, each neatly labelled. She made discreet and imaginative use of flowers, some of which stood in pencil-thin vases. She had lately taken up dressmaking, bending her head low as she worked, absorbed and oblivious, it seemed, of the century. She read a great deal and enjoyed being alone; she was a self-sufficient person.

'You should mix more,' Colin would say encouragingly. 'Make new friends.'

'No thank you,' she would reply. 'I'm perfectly happy.'

She did not care what the neighbours thought; they were graceless, imitative creatures.

Physically she was on the small side, with clear blue eyes that gave life a challenging look. She had a sensuality that pleased and excited men. It was in her quick, bold way of walking, those challenging eyes, the roundness of her breasts. There had been many lovers before her marriage, but none since. It wasn't that she particularly believed in faithfulness after marriage; it was simply that the question had not arisen.

Sometimes she felt her life was being held in suspension. Her lonely walks, her sewing, the curl of smoke from Colin's pipe, were like ambiguities in a language she understood only sketchily. They were more than they seemed, yet their real meaning was denied her. It gave her a dreamy sense of possibilities, so that small things achieved significance. There was an old stone bridge down a country lane and she would stand there, looking at the water swirling below. The river had an oily, lugubrious look, yet sometimes she imagined she saw fish dart and glide. And once she really did see a kingfisher. It had thrilled her, this electric blue light skimming the water. She had told no-one about it; it was something exclusive to herself, one of the signs and portents that gave her hope. One day release would come. It was simply a matter of survival.

Just across the bridge was an empty cottage, neglected and forlorn. She had once suggested buying it and doing it up, but Colin had scoffed. 'It would cost us a fortune to modernise that old heap,' he said complacently, as if the assessment were itself a matter for self-congratulation. But she did not want to 'modernise' at all. She would have waved a magic wand to conjure up the original and live there alone in a remote past, when the river ran clear and the kingfisher skimmed the electric-blue water. Their house in Hollybush grated on her; the whole place was a horror. The clipped, middle-class hedges, the rattle and whine of the lawnmowers, the husbands cutting the grass or washing their cars with an air of colour-supplement virtue, all these made her want to throw up.

One afternoon she found builders at work on the cottage. One of them wolf-whistled and she hurried past, confused and dismayed. It was all over, her idyll. Oh, *why* hadn't they bought it? By the time she reached home she had worked herself up to a fine pitch of resentment. 'What on earth's wrong with you?' Colin demanded, but she would not say. Obscurely she felt that to do so would be to lose the place twice over.

She went back there in a better mood, curious to see what was happening. The roof was being re-slated, while a concrete mixer gulped and churned away. Who would move in there when all this was finished? She pictured a vigorous couple, thirtyish like herself, busily creating the perfect garden; pictured them with self-lacerating candour, he cheerfully humping barrowloads of clods and weeds, she pausing to push a stray lock of fair, pre-Raphaelite hair from her glowing brow. She hated them on sight.

'What do you think?' she asked carelessly that evening. 'Someone's bought the cottage.'

'What cottage is that?' Colin murmured; he was reading.

'There's only one cottage.'

He looked up. 'That one by the bridge, you mean? Bloody fools.'

'We could have got it for ourselves. Done it up as we wanted.'

'We didn't want to though, did we?'

'*You* didn't want to, you mean.'

12

'What's all this? Not blaming me, are you?'

'Oh no, Colin,' she said sarcastically. 'I'd never blame you for anything.'

'What's that supposed to mean?'

'Nothing.'

'Well then.' He turned a page. 'They'll be sorry, I reckon. Cost them a bomb.'

'You're an architect, aren't you?' she retorted. 'You could've kept the price down.'

He smiled faintly. 'You'd need more than an architect for that, Kate. You'd need a bloody miracle.'

She stared at him, so cool, so complacent, so hideously *right*, and wondered if it had always been like this, for by now she could not remember.

2

The builders worked fast. Soon it was hard to recall what the place had been like before. The roof was retiled, there were new windows and doors, and an extension blended (almost) perfectly with the original cottage. The men were used to her now and the wolf whistles had given way to neighbourly smiles. There was a panache about one of them that she found appealing; it made the efforts of the others look crabbed and diffident. They exchanged words briefly as he was leaving one afternoon, after throwing some gear into the back of a van.

'Nice day for a walk,' he ventured.

'Yes, it is.' She stopped, half-smiled. 'Got much more work to do on this?'

'Not a lot. Couple more weeks.'

'It looks nice.'

'Pretty good. Fancy living there yourself?'

She hardly paused. 'No, not really,' she lied. 'I'm quite happy where I am.'

He gave her a quizzical look, as if he wasn't sure whether to believe her.

''Bye now,' she said shortly, feeling caught out and irritated. Why had she spoken to him at all? She avoided the place for several days, and never saw him again.

They went on holiday and when they returned the cottage was finished. It stood there in the thin rain of a

September morning, waiting. Its stillness was strange after the bustle of the builders. She had a sense of being watched as she stood on the bridge, looking at the eddies and ripples below. That evening she was filled with a strange happiness. It was as though something inside her had been fulfilled.

'Ah,' he said, reading the *Cardiff Voice.* 'So that's who's bought it.'

'What?'

'The cottage. *Your* cottage,' he said mischievously.

'I haven't got a bloody cottage.'

'Well, the one you fancied.'

'You mean it's in there? Who's bought it?'

'Guess.'

'How can I possibly? Give it here.' She reached out.

'No. Guess.'

'Don't be so infuriating, Colin. Tell me.'

'Have a guess. You ought to be able to.'

His black hair clung close to his scalp, as if glued to it. She was acutely aware of this, and of the stupid grin on his face.

'Why should I? Is it somebody famous?'

'*Was* famous. Somebody you admire.'

'I don't admire anyone. Give it to me, Colin.'

'No, you have to guess.' He clutched the paper to him. 'Come on, Kate. You can do it. I'll give you a clue. A writer.'

'A *writer*. Coming to live here?'

'In your cottage.'

'Don't keep saying that!'

'Oh, sorry. T.S.'

'T. S what?'

'That's his name. T.S. something.'

'Eliot?' she ventured sarcastically.

15

'He's dead.'

'So's everyone else round here. He should feel at home.'

'You ought to get it, Kate,' he said placatingly. 'You've read all his novels.'

'*Novels.* Don't know any T.Ses.'

'Yes you do. Think on, Kate. Think . . . angry.'

'Angry.' Her eyes widened. 'Not Ted Sloane.'

'Duh-ruh!' he fanfared.

'I don't believe it. Give me a look.'

'No,' he teased. 'I'm reading it.'

'Give it to *me*, Colin,' she said dangerously.

He handed it to her. His eyes gleamed with something that could have been malice. 'I didn't know he was still alive. He must be a hundred at least.'

She did not hear him, absorbed as she was in the story.

'The bastard,' she breathed.

'Not very nice, is it?'

'Nice? He ought to be shot.'

I can exclusively reveal, wrote Simon Gregg in his gossip column, *that a world-famous author – or should that be <u>once</u> world-famous? – has come to live in our midst. He is none other than Ted Sloane, one of the Angry Young Men school of the 1960-ish vintage. The vintage has, alas, long gone sour and Mr Sloane's reputation is not what it was.*

He is now installed in a renovated cottage in the swish suburb of Hollybush, far removed in spirit – as well as geographically – from the 'sodden and unkind Midlands' where he spent his formative years before spiralling into all too brief success.

I paid him a visit yesterday to extend the hand of friendship but, sad to say, the sometime Angry Young

Man has grown no less angry with the passing of the years. In fact, he shut the door in my face.

One can only conclude that Mr Sloane is anxious to avoid being mobbed by his dwindling band of admirers. Or perhaps he simply has nothing to say.

'Damn cheek,' fumed Kate. 'That's libellous, isn't it?'

'I'd say it was, yes.'

'Who's he think he is anyway, writing about Ted Sloane like that? He isn't fit to wipe his boots.'

'Exactly.' Colin, who had no love for the *Voice* after its knocking of one of his buildings, tapped gungy end-bits of pipe tobacco into the ashtray. 'But why's he come to live here? That's the point.'

'Yes.' She frowned. 'I wonder.'

'He hasn't written anything for years, has he? What's the last book he brought out?'

'*August Darkness,*' she said instantly.

'It bombed, didn't it?'

'It did *not*. It was a bloody good book.'

'Yes, but it didn't sell well though, did it? You told me so yourself. That's why he stopped writing.'

'Did I say that?'

'Yes, you did.'

'Well,' she said stoutly. 'He'd made his reputation by then. Maybe that's why he stopped . . . But just think of it, Colin – living here!'

'In your cottage,' he said impishly. 'You see? If we'd bought it he wouldn't be living there now. It was fate.'

'Bugger off,' she said without rancour.

Colin, yellow pouch in lap, was stuffing his pipe with tobacco again.

'And if you're going to stink the place out,' she said, more spiritedly, 'you can go somewhere else.'

17

'I'll go to my den if you like,' he offered. But he lit up where he was and she appeared not to notice.

Ted Sloane, she kept repeating inside herself. Ted Sloane. Was he really out there, living in her cottage? If so, anything was possible.

3

It was easy to be a bookworm in Cork because there were so many books to feed on. At fifteen, Kate Mallin devoured books as her friends devoured pop magazines and singles. She had her favourite second-hand bookshops, where she guzzled happily and bought what she could afford. The name Ted Sloane meant nothing to her at first. She took the novel from the shelf, *The Sound of Betrayal*, because of its title. She flicked idly through the pages, then was hooked.

'What are you reading now?' her mother asked indulgently.

Kate flipped the book over to show her the cover.

'Ted Sloane,' her mother murmured. 'The name's familiar.'

'It's brilliant, Mother. Have you read him?'

'No, can't say I have. What's it about?'

'A girl and an older man – running away together.'

'Ho! Hope it doesn't give you any ideas.'

'It's terrific. I'm going to read all his other books.'

'Well, don't tell your father. He might get worried.'

The Sound of Betrayal, Wings of Mourning, Eden's Rock, August Darkness . . . She got them through the library, the last with difficulty. There were four only.

What she liked in them was the passion, the vigour of the writing, the protagonists (all the same male, ingeniously reinvented), the gripping storyline. Why had he stopped writing?

19

She asked her English teacher at school. 'Oh – him,' was the dismissive reply. 'One of the Angries. They didn't have much to say. Don't waste your time on them.'

Angries? she had asked. What were they?

'Angry young men, so-called,' replied Sister Veronica. 'People who thought a lot of themselves and not much of anyone else.'

That surely went for a lot of writers, thought Kate privately. It did not affect her judgement of Ted Sloane in the least.

Later, much later, there was a programme on television about John Osborne, John Braine, Alan Sillitoe and the rest. Osborne appeared in it, bearded now, railing about the futile theatre of the 80s, and Braine was there too, like Sillitoe still writing novels. There was grainy old film showing Ted Sloane talking to Huw Wheldon in *Omnibus*, and cheap jibes about his disappearance from the scene altogether, into a literary black hole perhaps. Kate had been furious. She had obtained all his novels by then, two with great difficulty. Her enthusiasm was unabated. She wished – how she wished – he had written more.

She first saw him at the supermarket. He was unmistakable: that leonine head, the proud Roman nose. It was the face that had looked at her from the dust jackets of his novels; the face she remembered from *Omnibus*. He was putting tins into a shopping basket and the action diminished him.

She felt she was in a movie. Selfconsciously she plucked goods from shelves and glanced around every so often to see where he was, afraid all the time that she might meet his eyes. What if they looked at each other? She could not acknowledge him, yet could not ignore him. She almost wished not to be there, yet shivered with excitement that she was. At the checkout she found herself two places behind him. She noticed everything, yet pretended she wasn't looking. He paid by cheque; as he bent over to write it, she could stare at him shamelessly. He had on an open-neck shirt, a jacket none too new, smart but far from designer jeans. After handing over the cheque he turned suddenly, as if aware of her gaze. She blushed deeply, stared down at the floor, feeling foolish.

Driving home in the little run-about Colin had bought her, she felt ashamed and vexed with herself. She was behaving like a schoolgirl! What was Ted Sloane to her? She said nothing to Colin that evening. What could she say? But that night she lay awake a long time, recalling every moment in minuscule detail. Especially she remembered the way he had turned suddenly. Why hadn't she looked back at him boldly? What harm would it have done? When at last she slept her dreams were confused and she woke up feeling tired and cross. She felt she must take a job, any job, simply to get out of the house, to fix her mind on something outside herself. Her obsession with Ted Sloane, yesterday's man, was symbolic of a deep sickness in herself. Yet when Colin left for work she felt the heaviness inside her as keenly as ever. She was useless, a woman who could not bear her husband children or do anything worthwhile; she was nothing.

The following day she felt better. Looking through the front picture window, she saw Councillor Denzil Parsons passing. Pink and plump, he symbolised the kind of Tory complacency she despised. Benignly he strode along, warmed by the September sun and his own sense of purpose. She did not mind him so much today, because she had other things on her mind.

It was one of those days that strike a perfect balance between summer and autumn. The air was still, as if the change of season required a momentary holding of breath. High summer lingered in the gardens, but the tired green of the trees was turning to rust. Kate walked briskly, bobbing along in red slacks and sweater. She turned a bend in the road and soon put the suburb behind her. It was stupid, how nervous she felt. Of course she wouldn't see him; why should she?

She thought of Colin on the train to London, poring over his wretched papers. Poor Colin. But why poor? He was successful, admired, while she . . . what was she? Impatiently she cast introspection aside.

There were blackberries in the hedgerow and she picked one or two of them, relishing the juice and the texture of the fruit in her mouth. When she came to a farm gate she rested her elbows on the top bar, gazing at the horses from the riding stable dipping their long, smooth heads into the grass. Sunlight glinted on the web a spider was spinning in the hedgerow, just a few feet away. Again she thought of Colin on the train, but now she felt a fierce exultation. She was free! Why tie herself down to a piffling little job?

Soon she was within sight of the cottage. Seized by sudden panic, she nearly turned back. But her legs seemed independent of her fears, carrying her forward so that there was nothing to do but go remorselessly on, the way she had gone so often and with such indifference.

Suddenly Ted Sloane appeared from around the side

of the cottage, pushing a wheelbarrow. The sight was so incongruous, so completely unexpected, that she almost stopped dead in her tracks. He had on old green cords, a khaki shirt, brown woollen gloves. All this she took in at a glance. Outwardly she remained calm, a respectable married woman taking a walk, while inside her heart was thumping, thumping.

He watched her pass. She had a feeling that his eyes were boring into her, but could have been mistaken.

She had bowed her head piously at prayer, as every good Catholic girl should. She had loved the ceremonies of the faith, the host lifted high at Mass, the priest reading from the Bible held up by the altar boy. She had striven hard to believe as her parents did, unquestioningly, irrefutably. But something escaped her, the ability to give herself entirely. The idea of the Virgin she found exalting, the sense of womanhood raised to unprecedented heights. 'Mary, blessed Mary,' she murmured. 'Mary, Mother of God.' She pictured the Virgin as she was portrayed in the stained-glass windows of the church where they worshipped, clothed in a long dress of magenta blue and with a golden halo coiled above her head. She found it easy to pray to her, asking her to intercede, yet was increasingly aware, as she grew into womanhood, that it was not intercession she required but acceptance by the Virgin herself. Jesus, to her, was a shadowy figure, doing busy things with his male companions, being a deity. The Virgin, to her, was – in spite of that halo – one whose humanity was merely of a different kind from her own. She felt that, if they met, she could talk to this woman, not of her Son nor of the complexities of religion but simply of the things in her life that bothered her. The Virgin, she knew, would have the answers.

'Did you have a good day?' Kate asked, as Colin uncorked a bottle of Australian red in the kitchen.

'Not bad at all. Looks as if we're going to get that Eaglefield contract.'

'Are you now? That should put a smile on Charlie's face.'

'I should say.' He splashed the wine carelessly into a couple of glasses, handed one to Kate. 'Might cheer the old bugger up for a minute anyway. *Skoal.*'

'*Skoal.*' She pushed a strand of hair away from her eyes. 'How's Matthew these days?'

'Oh, not bad. Miserable as sin of course, but what do you expect?'

'No sign of them making it up?'

'Don't think so. Gone too far for that, I think.'

'Pity.' Stirring the casserole, sipping the wine then putting the glass down, looking so poised, so feminine, so *right*, she filled Colin with a sense of well-being and pride. How had he managed to get a wife like this, a full ten years younger than himself? And keep her?

'And you?' he enquired.

'Oh, all right.' She hesitated, then said diffidently, 'I happened to see Ted Sloane.'

'The famous author!' he said brightly. 'Where?'

'Oh, just outside his house. He was in the garden.'

'Writing a best-seller in the rose bushes?'

'Don't be silly. Anyway, it's not the time of year for roses.'

'Well, don't keep me in suspense. What did he say?'

'Nothing. Why should he?'

'Oh. How disappointing. I thought he might have . . .'

'What?'

'Oh, I don't know. Talked about his novels.'

'Oh, yes. Very likely.'

She was slightly flushed, vexed with herself for mentioning the meeting. It made it seem more important than it was.

'Of course, it's his own fault,' said Colin suddenly.

'What is?' asked Kate, startled.

'He was playing around, wasn't he? No wonder she went off him.'

She realised he meant his colleague, Matthew Slater, and was surprised by the relief she felt that he had dismissed the subject of Ted Sloane so easily.

'Maybe he had good reason to,' she said lightly.

Colin frowned. 'There's never a good reason.'

Prude, she thought, wanting to chaff him and then remembering the presumed cause of his puritanism, the errant father who had gone off with another woman before returning, ineffectually.

'Why don't you sit down and relax?' she said. 'This'll be ready in a minute.'

'I'm quite happy here, thank you,' he replied complacently, still standing there with the glass in his hand.

She felt the old irritation squirm under her skin. It made her hot and she was hot enough already, in this kitchen with an overwhelming husband who would not give her space.

'I'm going to dish up in a minute, Colin. I need some *room*.'

'Oh, I'm sorry,' he said huffily and retreated.

Damn damn *damn*. Damn damn *damn*. Damn damn

damn. She clumped the food onto the plates and carried them into the living-room, where Colin smiled sweetly and she knew herself to be forgiven. Tears of mingled rage and frustration prickled behind her eyes.

That night she made love savagely and he was filled with triumph, his semen pumping into her as she groaned and dug her nails into his back. He knew the effect he had on her and was at once exalted and fearful. He might so easily lose her. She was capricious, unpredictable.

Afterwards he slept heavily while she lay awake, peopling the darkness. Martin was there, fumbling with her brassiere till she pushed him away gently and undid it herself. A gentle, breathless boy, too keen not to harm her to do her any good. Then Carl, a seducer so willing to be seduced in return. And then her mother dying of cancer.

Oh God. Oh Mary, Mother of God. Oh Mary.

She slept at last, one arm wrapped around Colin, her face snuggled into his back like that of an innocent.

4

It edged up to Kate like an unpleasant if not dangerous animal. By Friday there was no ignoring the dinner party she'd arranged.

It was not the preparation she disliked but the actual playing of hostess. She loathed the demands it made on her to be polite, interested, the kind of social being she did not wish to be. But she had to do it for Colin's sake. It was expected of her.

There were four guests that evening, Philip Carver and his wife, Margaret, and Sir Charles and Lady Celia Lewis. Carver was Head of Admin. with the BBC in Cardiff, an Englishman whose connections were presumed to reach out in many directions, and thus someone it was useful for Colin to cultivate. Sir Charles, on the other hand, was a man to soft-soap for more immediate reasons, as boss of the architectural firm that employed him. Their wives provided a study in contrasts: Margaret Carver affected a sophisticated, tired languor, sharpened occasionally by a viperish observation, while Lady Lewis sported the bright naiveté of one who had long ago decided that an unspoilt-Valleys-girl persona suited her best. Kate told herself there were far worse social pretensions, and resigned herself to navigating the waters of a fairly predictable evening.

It was soon evident, however, that unexpected gusts might ruffle the surface. They came first in the guise of a discussion on the ethics of the Gulf War, which Sir Charles had firmly supported.

'It's time Saddam Hussein was given his come-uppance,' he asserted. 'The pity is we didn't finish him off.'

'There was no mandate to do that,' argued Margaret Carver. 'The UN's job was simply to turf him out of Kuwait.'

'The UN!' sneered Sir Charles. 'Useless lot of poofs. They should have left it to us and the Yanks.'

'Poofs?' Margaret frowned. 'What have poofs got to do with it?'

'I think you've both got a point,' put in Colin quickly. 'It's absurd that Saddam should still be in power but on the other hand –'

'It's not just absurd, it's disgusting,' Sir Charles said. 'The man's a monster. He's got weapons of mass destruction. He's –'

'Unlike us and the Americans, of course,' said Margaret with a brittle smile.

'What?'

'We don't have weapons of mass destruction, do we?'

'Well,' huffed Sir Charles after a moment. 'We certainly don't stockpile chemical weapons or gas our own people.'

'Don't we?'

'Not to my knowledge, no. My dear Margaret –'

'I think we have to get rid of him in other ways,' Carver said diplomatically. 'I don't honestly think the UN could have advanced on Baghdad.'

'Why not?'

'Because they had no mandate, as Margaret said.'

'Mandate! I'm old enough to remember Suez. Don't talk to me about mandate.'

'Oh, do stop talking politics!' tweeted Lady Lewis. 'Kate, that was absolutely delicious.'

Colin's relief was palpable. Sir Charles looked disgruntled. Carver retained his mandarin inscrutability. The talk, over coffee and After Eight Mints, turned to literary matters.

'Oh! I never read books these days,' said Lady Lewis comfortably. 'I get all the fiction I need from the TV soaps.'

'I get mine from reading the local rag,' scoffed Sir Charles. 'It gets worse every day.'

'Oh, get away with you,' said his wife. 'You've got your nose in it every evening. Honestly!' she appealed to the room in general.

'That doesn't mean I believe everything they say. Do you know, there was something in there the other day . . .' He launched into a rambling account of a report on local planning which made Kate's eyes glaze with boredom. She was startled into life by Margaret.

'They were right about one thing anyway,' she was saying. 'Did you see that piece in the gossip column the other day? Ted Sloane's come to live here.'

'Ted who?' enquired Sir Charles.

'Sloane. The author.'

'Never heard of him.'

Margaret gave him a swift, demolishing glance before turning to Kate. 'You have, I'm sure. Do you know his books?'

'Yes, I've got them all.'

'*Got* them. I must borrow them some time. You don't even see them in the library these days.'

'Of course,' said Kate, more willingly than she felt. Lending books, she knew, was equivalent to throwing them into the sea.

'Would somebody please tell me what this man writes?' asked Sir Charles, with the baffled look of one prepared to humour all sorts of peculiar tastes.

'Novels,' explained Colin promptly. 'He was one of the Angry Young Men school of writing back in the Sixties.'

'Even earlier than that,' corrected Margaret. 'They started in the late Fifties, if I'm not very much mistaken.'

'Good Lord!' exclaimed Sir Charles. 'What do you want with people like that then? You should be looking to the future!'

'I quite agree,' said Colin unctuously. 'I think they were all overrated anyway.'

He noted Kate's contemptuous glance, and prepared for warfare later.

'I remember them,' Lady Lewis put in unexpectedly. 'They were all about blood and gore, weren't they? People being beaten up in back streets and all that.'

'Not really,' said Kate.

'They were much of a muchness,' said Carver quietly. 'Except *The Outsider*. I thought that was brilliant.'

'Colin Wilson,' murmured Kate.

'What's he doing here though – Ted Sloane?' asked Colin.

'Ah,' said Margaret, looking at her husband significantly.

'Do you know, then?' asked Kate.

'Well.' Carver cleared his throat. 'It's only what people are saying, of course.'

Kate broke the silence. 'Well, what *are* they saying?'

'It's all hearsay,' said Carver diffidently. 'There may be nothing in it.'

'Oh go on Philip, do,' interposed Margaret impatiently. 'It's not as if you're making a statement to the press.'

'I should think not,' her husband said stiffly. 'This concerns the Other Side. Well, the story is that he's come here to write a soap. For Cambrian.'

'Ted Sloane? Writing a soap?' said Colin incredulously. 'Well, my God.'

'It doesn't bear thinking about, does it,' said Margaret gloomily. 'The things some people stoop to.'

'But is it true?'

'Looks like it,' Carver confirmed. 'Only don't quote me on it, will you?'

'Well, good heavens,' Colin exclaimed.

'I'd need some convincing,' said Kate quietly.

'But it's so exciting,' protested Lady Lewis. 'A TV writer – here!'

'He lives just up the road from us,' said Colin mischievously. 'You could get his autograph, Celia.'

'Oh, could I? No – you get it for me, Colin!'

'I don't know what all the fuss is about,' grumbled Sir Charles. 'I wouldn't look at it anyway – I can't stand television. Complete waste of time.'

'Oh – you.' His wife flapped a dismissive hand.

That night, undressing, Kate felt the house closing in on her; she could almost hear the walls moving. Listening to Colin gargling in the bathroom, she was overwhelmed with a sense of unreality. What was she doing here? Who was she? She wanted to rush out of the room, out of the house, flee somewhere, anywhere. She fought back the panic attack by repeating a mantra she had used during her breakdown. 'I-am-not-*me,* I-am-not-*I,* I-am-not-*he,* I-am-not-*she.*' She was a stone, a cloud, a plant in the desert, a hoop being bowled along by a child dressed in old-fashioned clothes. She was sexless, ageless, nerveless. The attack subsided as she rushed into her nightie and slumped into bed, pulling the blankets up over her head. The bathroom door closed, Colin padded back into the bedroom. She felt him looking at her. She prayed he would not speak.

He got into bed, switched off the bedside lamp. Her back was towards him. He cleared his throat. 'Enjoy the evening?' he asked.

'No.'

'Oh? Why's that then?'

'You know why. I hate it. All of it.'

'We won't do it again if you don't want to.'

'You have to though, don't you?'

'I don't *have* to, Kate.'

He was lying on his back. His soft breathing, in and out, in and out, filled Kate with inexplicable rage. 'What didn't you like particularly?' he asked mildly.

'I'm going to *sleep,* Colin.'

'Was it me?'

'Why should it be you?' she asked, startled.

'Well . . . I don't think you like me very much these days.'

She tensed, her rage dissipated by the sheer unexpectedness of his words. 'What makes you say that?'

'It's obvious.'

'Oh, Colin,' she said, turning. 'Don't.'

'Don't tell the truth?' he asked, his mouth twisting in the darkness.

'It's not.' She ran a finger down the side of his face. 'It's really not.'

'Don't pretend, Kate,' he said wearily.

'It's me, love,' she said softly. 'Not you. I'm useless. You'd be better off with someone else.'

'You would, you mean.'

'No . . . *no.*'

Her finger moved up and down his cheek; then touched his lips. He was motionless. She felt a stirring inside her; pity and love for him intermingled. What were his irritating ways beside this longing for him? She wanted him; had always wanted him. 'Please, darling,' she murmured.

He shook his head, muttered something incomprehensible. She lay across him, running her tongue across the black V of hair on his chest. Unlike her, he slept naked. He wanted to reject her but could not.

Over breakfast she said: 'I'm going to get a job. I want to do something with my life.'

'You are doing something.' He smiled smugly. 'Forgotten already?'

'I don't know why you put up with me,' she said, ignoring this scarcely-veiled reference to their love-making. 'All I do is make you miserable.'

'I'm not miserable.' He splashed milk over his muesli. 'I'm the happiest man alive.'

'Don't pretend, Colin. You know what you said last night.'

'I was in a bad mood,' he said lightly. 'I was tired.'

'You meant it though, didn't you?' she said seriously. 'You think I don't like you.'

His tone changed. 'You don't though, do you?'

'No. Sometimes I don't. But that doesn't stop me loving you.'

'Pretty heavy stuff, isn't this? For breakfast time.'

'Just as well to have it out though, isn't it?'

'Save it up, Kate. I've got to go to work.'

'No. Let's do it now.'

'What?' he asked, startled.

'Tell me what you think of me. *Really* tell me.'

'For God's sake, Kate. Give over.'

'Do you think I'm weak? I know I am. I'm hopeless.'

'*Please.*'

'I can't give you any children and don't bring any money into the house. I bitch at you and make you mad at me. I know all this, Colin. I know it.'

'I don't want to *hear* all this, Kate –'

'You said the truth last night. I don't like you very much. I hate the way you fawn over your repulsive boss. I hate your smelly pipe and all sorts of things. But I love you.'

'Jesus *Christ.*'

'Go on, then. Get mad at me. Hit me. Do something.'

'I don't want to hit you. Shut *up*, Kate.'

'Don't you? Don't you?'

'Hell's bells.' He stood up suddenly, his chair clattering to the floor. 'I'm going.'

'That's right, go. Cop out of it, as usual.'

He thumped upstairs, turned the cold tap on full, stood over the basin, staring, staring.

When he went back down, he said: 'Look, Kate. It doesn't matter to me whether you get a job or not. It's not important.'

'Isn't it?' She was staring at the blank TV screen.

'No. You haven't been well. When you're better . . .'

'Pigs might fly,' she said with a strange, crooked smile.

'I love you,' he said. 'That's what matters. That's all that matters.'

He bent and kissed her. Her lips were cold.

Sitting before that silent TV, she drifted into sleep, exhausted by the emotions of the morning. She had a strange, disturbing dream about a wild animal threatening her: some kind of badger, but such a badger as no naturalist would have recognised. It was in a fight with another of its species, their sharp teeth rending one another pitifully. Its opponent gained the upper hand so that in the end it was imprisoned by people who were much vaguer in her dream than the beasts. They suspended the creature in a pit, its teeth sunk into some object. She woke suddenly. It was only half-past ten.

She left the house impatiently, forgetting her coffee date with next-door neighbour, Joyce, at eleven. It did not matter now; she had to get away from the house, away from herself, ideally. Inexorably she walked the lane towards the cottage. Ted Sloane was nowhere to be seen. She looked boldly at the house and its surroundings. The garden was much tidier now and smoke drifted up from the chimney. For the first time she realised that for all the work that had gone into it, the cottage still had no garage.

The dog appeared suddenly, from around a bend in the lane, bounding up to her noisily. She did not mind barking dogs, especially one as friendly as this. She crouched down, patting the black spaniel and making reassuring noises. 'Trinder! Come here!' its master commanded, hurrying towards her. 'You bad dog. Come here!'

'It's all right,' she assured him, hardly daring to look up. 'I like dogs. Really.'

'He shouldn't *do* that. He's getting into very bad habits.' His voice was blue, dark blue, not at all the voice she'd remembered from the telly.

35

'No you're not. Are you, boy?' The dog, noisily panting, thrashing its tail joyously, was entirely won over.

He stood looking down at them, frowning. 'I've seen you somewhere before, haven't I?'

'I don't know. Have you?' she said, feigning indifference . She dared not look up at him.

'You live round here, do you?' he asked gruffly.

'Yes. In the village.'

'Village!' he scoffed. 'It's a suburb, isn't it?'

'People call it the village though.'

'That's as may be. But it doesn't make it one.' There was the faintest smear of Brummie in his voice. She wanted to hold on to this moment, to be near her idol.

'Well. . . Come on then, Trinder.'

The spaniel began barking, wanting to stay with her to be fussed over for ever.

'Trinder! For God's sake. I'm sorry about this,' he said, leaning over so that he was near her, so near she could – if she dared – have touched him.

'Don't apologise. It's all right – really.'

'Bloody silly animal.' He dragged the dog away by its collar.

'Goodbye, Trinder,' said Kate, surrendering reluctantly.

At the gate he paused. 'I remember. It was in Asda's, wasn't it?'

'That's right.' She nearly added 'Ted', but something stopped her just in time. He gave her a long look, then turned and went through the gate. Impulsively she said, 'We nearly bought this house, you know.'

'Did you?' He paused, surprised. 'Who's we?'

'Colin and me – my husband.'

'Then why didn't you?'

'He thought it'd be too much – doing it up.'

He smiled, and suddenly his whole bearing seemed youthful. 'Wise man. It's costing me a fortune.'

'You like it here though – don't you?' she hazarded.

'Oh yes – it's fine.' He hesitated, as if about to say more, then drew back into himself. 'Ah well. Good day to you. Sorry about the dog.'

'It's all right – really.'

He went briskly up the path. She resumed her walk, hearing the door close behind him as she rounded the bend from which he had emerged so unexpectedly.

5

'Damn!' Yvonne Morris exploded. She was just beginning to get the hang of the computer; and now this! The blank screen, suddenly wiped clean of images, stared back at her unblinkingly. She slapped both hands down hard on the desk in her vexation. Her fingers tingled, but the screen remained indifferent. There was something wrong with this damned machine; they'd have to get her a new one.

Yvonne, dark-complexioned, black-haired and with eyebrows more prominent than she would wish, was not conventionally pretty but had a liveliness that made up for this. Her expressive features gave her a vivacity which, with her erect posture and shapely breasts, made her a more attractive figure than she might otherwise have been. In her mid-twenties, she had the confidence that comes with money and a sound private education. The Morrises, though not wealthy, had been able to afford to give their only daughter what they thought of as 'a good start in the world.' They rarely admitted it even to themselves, but were slightly disappointed that she had not made more of this. Her secretarial job with the Charles Lewis Partnership, although not to be sneezed at, fell far short of the prospects they had visualised for her.

Yvonne, alone in the office – an infrequent occurrence – looked over the grey mudflats of Cardiff's old dockland and wondered what it would be like when the long-awaited barrage had created the artificial lake that existed, at present, only on the drawing board. The sooner the better, in her opinion. She found the present prospect uninviting, the desolation of the scene not enlivened in the least in winter by the visitations of rare birds that so excited the naturalists. The barrage might, with luck, make the scene as inviting as the marina in her native Swansea; she was enough of a Swansea Jack to regard many of its attractions as superior to Cardiff's, although she preferred the sophistication and liveliness of the rapidly-changing capital to the more down-market energy of Wales's second city.

Her reverie was interrupted by the appearance of an older woman, who looked surprised at the inactivity. 'Where they to then?' she asked in a harsh, sheet-metal voice. 'Gone ashore for a loaf, have they?' Sharon West's earthy witticisms did not always strike a chord with Yvonne, but now she smiled and inclined her head towards an inner room from which voices drifted indistinctly through the partition. 'Meeting,' she said laconically.

'Oh God. What's it this time, Eve?'

'Eaglefield.'

'Oh. That lot.' Sharon had dropped the exaggerated Cardiff accent which was a kind of self-mockery. 'Glad I'm not in on it.'

'Why?' Yvonne asked curiously.

'*Why?* Don't have to ask, do you?'

'It's only another job, isn't it?'

'Give over, Yvonne. You know what they're like as well as I do. Smart-arse suits looking for a quick profit.'

Yvonne inspected her well-manicured nails. 'That's

what it's all about, isn't it?' she murmured. 'Everybody's in it for the money.'

'Don't get all cynical on me, pet. I'm having a bad day.'

Yvonne, put out slightly by the patronage in Sharon's voice, did not answer. Instead she dialled an internal number. 'Can you spare a minute, Mike? This computer's playing up again . . . Yes, I've *tried* that . . . OK, OK . . . Thanks.' She sighed deeply.

Sharon, fortyish, her once-pretty face now veiled by a hard sheen of disillusion, looked pensively at the younger woman. 'Colin's in there, I suppose?'

'Yes, of course. It's his job, isn't it?' said Yvonne edgily.

'Mm. Rather him than me.'

'So you keep saying.'

'Doesn't seem to mind it, does he?' drawled Sharon. 'Funny, that.'

'Why funny?'

'Well, he's such a talented chap. You'd think this kind of job would bore the pants off him. Yet another office conversion! Jeez, we've got enough to last a lifetime already.'

'I don't suppose he'd got much choice,' replied Yvonne, with forced carelessness. 'If Charlie wants him to do it . . .'

'Exactly! Charlie snaps his fingers and Colin jumps.'

Yvonne, deeply irritated, was saved from the need to reply by the arrival of Mike, the CAD technician. An anorak to the core, he immersed himself in the problems of her computer. Sharon drifted back to the office she shared with him. Yvonne regained her composure.

The voices on the far side of the partition kept up their steady murmuration until the door opened and the foursome stepped through: Sir Charles, pinkly self-satisfied, Colin, relaxed and smiling, and the two businessmen from the Eaglefield Corporation. They swept through the office, laughing at a jest from Sir Charles and ignoring Yvonne and Mike, leaving in their wake an awkward silence.

Mike, the computer problem almost sorted, squinted a sly look at Yvonne. 'Good of you to help me, Mike,' she said coolly, with ineffable self-possession.

'I knew you wouldn't come, I just knew it,' complained Joyce.

'I'm sorry,' said Kate penitently.

'I left it till half-past and then I thought, bugger it, I'll have a coffee on my own. Where were you anyway?'

'I went for a walk.'

'*Walk*. You're always going for bloody walks. You'll walk your legs off one day, you'll see.' She pushed a straggly lock of her blonde hair back from her pink, glossy face. 'Which way'd you go?'

'Oh, just down towards the river,' said Kate casually.

'You're always going that way. Anyone'd think you'd got a lover down there.' Joyce sniggered.

'I should be so lucky.' Kate fought down the incipient blush. 'I like it there. It's interesting.'

'*Interesting*. You sound like a bloody teacher.'

She poured tea from a brown china pot into two mugs, one of which was adorned with woolly cartoonist's sheep against a background of Welsh Valleys terraced housing crazily climbing an impossibly steep hill. She gave the other, plainer one to Kate.

41

'How's that man of yours anyway?' she asked, settling herself opposite in the kitchen-cum-breakfast room.

'Oh, OK.'

'Don't see much of him, do you?'

'Yes I do,' answered Kate, surprised. 'I see a lot of him. Why do you say that?'

'Oh, I don't know. He's always off pretty early, isn't he? And he doesn't come back too soon neither, from what I can see.' She gave Kate a mischievous glance.

'You seem to spend a lot of your time looking at him,' said Kate acidly.

'Can't help it, can I? I see his car go down the road. It's big enough, God knows.'

'It's a company car.'

'Very nice. Wish we had one.'

'Derek's got one, hasn't he?'

'Oh aye. But it's his own company, isn't it? If you can call it that.'

Kate wondered, not for the first time, why she bothered coming in here to talk to this loud, gossipy woman who was always looking for some way through her defences.

'That reminds me,' Joyce went on. 'He's got a vacancy coming up soon. Receptionist. Fancy that?'

'No thank you.'

'Why not? It's a nice little number. Just getting people to fill up forms for having their teeth filled by Derek.'

Kate did not respond.

'Well, he told me to ask. He'd like to have you working for him. See a lot more of you then, wouldn't he?'

'I daresay he would,' said Kate carefully.

'Colin wouldn't mind, would he? It'd get you off his hands a bit, if you see what I mean.'

'No, I don't.' Kate gave her a straight look.

'Well . . . you'd be bringing home some lolly, wouldn't you? Not that that's the most important thing. It'd be good for you, wouldn't it?

'You mean I'm a lazy little bitch, do you?'

'No! Good God no! I'm only trying to help, that's all. I mean – you haven't been very well, have you?'

'I'm right as rain, Joyce. Only I just can't be bothered.'

'Don't be silly.' She bit her lip. 'I'm sorry – I know I'm interfering. But we're a bit worried about you both.'

'Well, don't be. We're all right. What makes you think we aren't, anyway?'

'Oh, nothing special. I'm sorry I spoke, Kate.' She tried to make light of it, getting up and floundering around. 'How about a slice of jam sponge, eh? Mam made it – it's really nice.'

'I don't think I can, thanks.'

'Oh, come on. Peace offering. Here.'

She put a slice on a plate and pushed it towards Kate, who stared at it indifferently.

'We're lucky, I suppose, with our two,' said Joyce cosily. 'They're a pain in the bum but they keep us going, at any rate.'

Going? thought Kate. Going where?

'Don't get me wrong,' Joyce rabbited on. 'We know you're fine together . . . but I suppose you've tried for a family, haven't you? It's just luck really.'

'We don't want a family,' lied Kate. 'We're quite happy as we are.'

'Oh, well – that's all right then. But –' A ring of the doorbell saved her the effort of wriggling free verbally. 'Who the hell can that be?' She hurried away and Kate ate the sponge hurriedly, seeing the interruption as a means of escape. The approach of a loud male voice filled her with dread. Its owner appeared in the doorway of the kitchen, hesitating as he saw Kate sitting there.

'You know Kate, don't you?' said Joyce, coming up behind him. 'My next-door neighbour. Kate, this is Brendan – you know each other, don't you?'

'Of course we do!' Brendan advanced, hand extended. 'Your Colin's wife, aren't you? He's got a twelve handicap, the bugger!' He smiled hugely, the very picture of senior citizen bonhomie, his silver hair a sheen of success above his Mr-Punch-like chops.

'Do sit down, Brendan,' said Joyce happily. 'We're just having a spot of tea.'

'No – I can't stay, bless you, just dropping these tickets in you asked for. I was passing this way so –'

'Oh, but you'll stay for a minute, won't you? We'll be glad of your company, won't we?' prattled Joyce, shooting a brittle, girls-together glance at Kate.

'I'd love to but I can't, really. I'm a busy man, you know – in spite of appearances. You're never so busy as when you're retired – you'll find that out, my dear, in good time.' Brendan's lugubrious voice rolled around the kitchen. 'I wonder how I ever found time to work – but then, you've got a long time to go, haven't you? How is your husband, anyway? I haven't seen him for a while.'

'He's fine, thanks,' clipped Kate, going as far as she might without snubbing him.

'Good, good. Do give him my regards, won't you? And tell him I'm practising hard, yes? Might give him more of a game next time!' He laughed, too loudly and for too long. 'Well, must be off now, Joyce, sorry I can't stop!'

Joyce followed him down the hall, still protesting at his too-soon departure. When she returned, Kate was on her feet.

'Oh, don't you go too! You've only just come!'

'Sorry, Joyce, I have to.'

'But why? You haven't –' She swallowed the words 'got anything to do' just in time. 'You know him, don't you?' she said quickly, taking a fresh tack. 'Him and his wife. Terrible pair!'

'Why terrible?'

Joyce's eyes widened in mock horror. 'You don't know? Really?'

'What, have they committed mass murder or something?'

'Worse! Far worse! They were swingers!'

'Swingers?'

'You know! Wild parties. Throwing car keys on the floor – that sort of thing!'

'Jesus.'

'Yes! They were notorious. You ask Colin.'

'How would he know?'

'He gets about more, doesn't he. They all know about it in the golf club. Half of them were up for it in the Sixties. Terrible time.' Her eyes glistened with the dreadfulness of it.

'I don't believe it. They're just stories.'

Joyce laughed, a peculiar half-shriek. She had a mad look, as if possessed. 'Just you ask Colin then, if you don't believe me. He's heard all the gossip as well, at the golf club. They were all at it in those days. Half of Cardiff.'

'I'm going,' said Kate. 'Thanks for the tea – and the cake. It was very nice.'

'I've offended you, haven't I? Just by telling the truth.'

'Don't be silly, Joyce. I'm not offended. Come over tomorrow, will you? I'm sorry about this morning.'

'You know what you are, don't you? You're a snob.' Joyce's face was contorted. 'You can't face up to life – that's your trouble.'

Kate stared at her, disbelieving her ears.

'Oh, go on then! If you must go.'

Kate swept past her.

'It's true – it's bloody true! Every word of it!'

Kate cut short her rant by banging the door behind her.

6

'It's OK as far as it goes,' said Ted Sloane. 'But it needs more.'

'Like what?' The question came from a dark-haired, round-bellied man of forty-plus wearing a black open-neck shirt, jeans and an earring.

'In a word, more body.'

'That's two words in my dictionary.'

Some of those at the script conference shuffled papers uneasily. Ted was unperturbed.

'I'm not blaming you entirely, Gwynne. The storyline's weak. And some of the characters are too clichéd.'

Gwynne Tecwyn glowered at him. 'I did some of the storylining myself. I'd like to know what's wrong with it, if you can spare the time.'

Ted looked at him calmly. 'Well, to begin with –'

'No – not now,' interrupted Carol Hart decisively. 'I've had enough for today. Thanks everyone. We'll resume tomorrow, ten-thirty.' She sent her sharp producer look gleaming round the table, clumped her scripts together and stood up. She was thin, pale, her cobalt-blue eyes made more prominent still by her mottled purple-and-silver glasses. Gwynne shot her a disgruntled glance, looked as if he might be about to say something, changed his mind and trundled from the room. Ted stayed where he was, with the tired, resigned look of a man misplaced but willing to see things out. As Carol spoke animatedly to the woman on her right he got up slowly, ambled to the window and stared out at the dusty, plaza-like area enclosed by three sides of Media City, HQ of Cambrian Television, independent television provider for Wales and the Marches. Ted Sloane was a tall man but stood slightly hunched, his posture confirming the impression he gave of one not entirely at ease with the situation. For all that he had a formidable appearance, his iron-grey, tightly-textured hair surmounting a broad forehead corrugated with deep, decisive lines. His large, boldly drawn face was dominated by a Roman nose but his eyes were his dominant feature: deep brown, unexpectedly liquid and with the capacity to disarm or unsettle the person he settled them on. He moved suddenly, almost shaking himself with a tremor parodying an action typical of his spaniel Trinder, and was going towards the door when Carol said, 'A word with you please, Ted, before you go. In my office, right?' Her quick smile came and went rapidly, scarcely breaking the attention she was giving her interlocutor. Ted nodded and made directly for an open door bearing the name-plate 'Carol Hart, Head of Drama.' He went inside and she swept in shortly afterwards. 'Shit,' she said unemotionally, closing the door behind her. Unabashed, he continued reading the *Guardian* he had taken from her desk. 'That man. Will be. The death of me,' she declared, staccato phrases punctuated by the lighting of a cigarette. Ted did not respond. 'Hell.' She slumped into the black mock-leather chair behind her desk.

'What's bothering you?' asked Ted idly.

'Everything. I shouldn't have brought you into this. I'm sorry.'

'Why? Don't you think I can do it then?'

'Of course you can do it. You can do it standing on your head. It's just that I shouldn't have asked you. It's self-indulgent.'

Ted put the paper down carefully. 'I wouldn't do it that way,' he said pensively. 'Not on my head.'

Carol glanced at him, irritated. 'The blood would rush so,' he added mildly.

'Dad,' said Carol. 'Up yours.'

'Thank you,' Ted replied graciously.

'Oh, bollocks,' said Carol wearily.

Ted looked at his daughter gravely. 'If you go on like this,' he observed, 'you're not going to make forty.'

'What makes you think I want to?'

'I'll be disappointed if you don't. I was hoping you'd take me out to dinner then to celebrate.'

'Some hopes. We'll still be sorting this lot out, by the look of things.'

'Trouble with you is, Carol, you worry too much. Come on. Let's get going.'

'No . . . no,' she protested. 'I brought you here to say something, Ted.'

'Well?'

She steadied herself. 'This asshole – Gwynne,' she said shortly. 'I'm getting rid of him.'

'What? Can you do that?'

'Yes. *Yes*. He was contracted for six storylines and the first two scripts. We've paid him. He can get lost.'

'And?'

'And what?'

'Who's going to do the scripts instead?'

'You are.'

'Oh no,' said Ted firmly, shaking his head.

49

'Yes.'

'Not in a million years, Carol.'

'*Yes*. Read my lips, Dad. Yes – yes – yes.'

'Read mine, girl. No-no-no.'

'You've got to do it, Dad.'

'No I haven't. And stop calling me Dad. It's not professional.'

'I don't care. You've got to do this for me.'

'Rubbish.'

'I mean it, Ted. You're the one to do it. You have to.'

Ted took a deep breath. 'Now look, Carol. You brought me in as script consultant. No more.'

'I know, but –'

'And that's the way it's going to be. Script consultant. Nothing else.'

'Things have changed, though –'

'Script consultant, Carol. Script *consultant*.'

'But you can do it, Ted. I know you can.'

'That's not the point. I don't want to.'

'You *have* to.'

'Don't keep saying that. I don't *have* to be here at all.'

'Oh, Dad – *Ted*. Hell – why can't I call you Dad in private?'

'You know why. Walls have ears.'

'But everybody knows who you are.'

'That's not the point. You know it's not.'

Carol stood up suddenly, scrunched out her half-smoked cigarette. 'Let's go eat. I'm hungry.'

'I'm not going to change my mind, Carol,' he warned.

'I don't expect you to. If you don't want to.' She gave him a quick, enigmatic glance.

'So how did it go?' asked Yvonne.

'Oh, so-so.' Colin stood in almost the exact position she had taken earlier, staring over the mudflats which had darkened considerably in the interim, as if sucking the dusk into themselves. In the middle distance Penarth Head was like the prow of a giant liner, its unseen passengers enlivening the dreary scene by switching on lights in their cabins.

'So they like what we're doing, do they?' Yvonne persisted.

'Mm?' He seemed, for a moment, to have forgotten she was there, then half turned, adding, 'Oh yes, they like it all right.'

Yvonne selfconsciously stood her ground, ready to leave the office but unwilling to do so until she had gained more from him than he had yet given her. Some moments passed, and gradually there seeped into the silence the realisation on his part that for some reason she was delaying her exit. 'What makes you think they don't, Yvonne?' he asked with a smile, a question directed not so much at her as himself as he wondered at her motive for staying, not yet willing to admit that it might be himself.

'Oh, I don't know. You can never tell with these people, can you?' She made a vague gesture, then smoothed down the coat she had donned some time before, prolonging the moment now to its ultimate stretching point.

'No,' he agreed, sudden interest in her and their situation bringing a strange look of incipient disbelief to his features. 'But I think we're pretty safe with this one.'

'I'm glad.' She risked a bright smile, her eyes meeting his. 'Make Charlie easier to live with, won't it?'

'Do you find him difficult?' asked Colin, animated now.

'No, not difficult but . . . well, he can be a bit prickly, can't he?' Yvonne, the beginnings of a hope she had never allowed herself giving her poise and assurance, held the steady look, daring him to glance away.

'Yes . . . but so can we all, I suppose. Ah well.' He broke the eye contact and yet, in spite of his dismissive tone, failed to disperse the atmosphere they had established. In moving towards the door he had to go in her direction, so they left the office side by side, and his new awareness of her gave his movements an untypical clumsiness. He left the neon lighting on for the cleaners who were already in the building, and together they went through the foyer into the brisk autumn evening.

'Well,' he said, hesitating, 'see you tomorrow, I suppose.'

'Yes. I suppose.' She stood by him, not moving, her eyes turned away now but her body close, receptive.

'You going anywhere this evening?' he asked casually.

'No. I've got nothing on at all.'

He was about to tear himself away when something, the slightest movement on her part, combined with the ambiguity of her words to wrench him out of his usual context.

'Would you like a drink – before you go?' he asked tentatively, in the manner of a man more than half expecting rejection.

She flashed him a smile. 'Yes. I would.'

'Right then,' he said, amazed. 'Let's go.'

It was late when Carol pulled up outside the cottage, at a point where the lane widened before narrowing again. Ted gave her a fatherly kiss before sauntering to the gate, lifting a hand in farewell. He paused a moment, looking up at the stars. There were no street lamps here to dilute any of their glitter.

As he opened the door, the dog bustled up to greet him. 'Good old Trinder, eh?' he murmured, digging his fingers into its springy coat. The dog whimpered joyfully, covering Ted's large face with huge, sloppy kisses. 'Been a good dog, eh? Course you have. One of the best, aren't you, Trinder?' The dog yelped its agreement. 'OK, old boy, quiet now. Let's sit down, shall we? I'm buggered.' Flopping onto the settee, Ted stretched out his long legs. Trinder squatted, looking up at him adoringly.

He had all but surrendered over dinner; only the formalities needed to be completed. He knew it; his daughter knew it; had he been asked, he would have agreed that even Trinder knew it. He had surrendered because, having given himself to the project, he had to do his damnedest to make it work; and that meant writing the whole caboodle himself.

'You can do it as Francis Kent if you like,' Carol had suggested when, knowing victory was hers, she had tried to soften the blow.

'Why should I do that?'

'Well, that's the name you used before, isn't it?'

He reflected briefly on his years as a TV scriptwriter, after the novels had dried up.

'No,' he said quietly. 'I'm not going back to all that. I'll do it as Ted Sloane or nothing.'

'That's OK by me,' Carol smiled. 'I just wondered, that's all.'

'Francis Kent is dead,' Ted said suddenly.

Like Mum, Carol found herself thinking.

He read her thoughts. Neither spoke. Psychic currents flowed unseen between father and daughter.

'I've done nothing as Francis Kent since your mother died,' murmured Ted. 'You know that, don't you?'

'No, I don't. I hadn't realised.'

He thought she might say more, but felt her withdraw from him – though not with the antipathy of yesteryear.

'There'll be stories, of course,' she remarked. 'In the papers.'

'Whoopee,' he returned laconically.

'But you never wanted it, did you?' she persisted. 'Publicity. You hated it – I know.'

'Long time ago, love. Water under the bridge.' The glib phrase lit up something in his mind: the river swirling under the bridge outside the cottage, the figure of a woman standing on it. Had he seen her there, or just imagined it?

'There's been something already anyway, remember?' he rushed on light-headedly. 'In the local rag. Nobody was interested, were they? Ted Sloane's a forgotten man. Thank God,' he added, almost as an afterthought.

'Yes . . . That horrible little piece in the *Voice*. How did they find out about you anyway?' she asked curiously.

'God knows. Someone at the estate agent's probably. Can't trust the bastards, can you?'

'And you say you're forgotten,' she said dryly.

'Forgotten enough, pet.'

The words returned to him now, repeating themselves like a train rhythm. 'Forgotten-enough . . . forgotten-enough . . . forgotten-enough . . .' They lulled him to the brink of sleep, till he was suddenly roused by an inner voice speaking his name, a voice he had heard only once and did not at first recognise. 'We nearly bought this house, you know,' it said. 'Colin and me.' The woman from Asda's! Why should he think of her? Awake now, he stood up. Trinder, tail wagging, looked up. 'Come on then, Trinder,' he said brusquely. 'Time for your constitutional.'

7

In defiance of the natural order of things, autumn was bringing Kate to life. The encounter with Ted Sloane, the argy-bargy with Joyce, even the intrusion of the ridiculous Brendan, provided a mix of sensations that made her more outward-looking than she had been for ages. Yet there was a tinge of uneasiness too: Joyce's spiky remark on Colin's long working hours, her scarcely-veiled hint that he might be up to something, was like a stone cast into still waters, the ripples widening for all her attempts to ignore them. Normally she would have thought nothing of his being even later home than usual, but with Joyce's malicious voice still knifing her she waited for the sound of his returning car with growing impatience.

It was gone nine when he at last strode into the house, with his usual cheery 'Hi!' Did she detect in it something forced that evening, and an unnatural glow in those so-blue, so-trusting eyes?

'What kept you?' she said snappily, ditching at once her determination to be ironical and detached, seeing an apparent indifference as the best way of probing his defences.

'I had a meeting,' he retorted. 'Why?'

'You're late, that's all. Very late. Anything could have happened to you.'

'Don't be silly.' He smiled, her over-the-top reaction letting him off the hook. 'It's not much later than usual. I never know when I'm going to finish, you know that.'

'You usually ring.'

'Well, I couldn't. The Eaglefield people were here. They insisted on going to the site again. You know what they're like.'

'No I don't. I don't know anything. I just sit here all day festering. I'm bloody fed up with it all.'

'Kate, darling!' He was all consideration, as she would have known he would be had she stopped to think, but she was beyond thought, her sudden suspicion of this model husband whose very perfection had been an irritant causing volcanic upheavals inside her.

'Look, I'm sorry. I should have rung, I know that, but I couldn't. I really couldn't. Oh, Kate.' And he too was amazed by the way he was behaving, for he had meant to tell her he had merely been having a social drink with his colleague Yvonne, for what harm was there in that? But Kate's whole jealous-wife demeanour had put the words out of reach, forcing him to respond in an instinctive, self-protective way which, even though he knew it put him in a false position, he found impossible to resist. So both, acting out of character, sparred with one another like marionettes in a crazy dance. She hid from him her chance encounter with Ted Sloane; he hid from her his illicit (as it was turning out to be) hour in the pub with Yvonne; without their knowing it, their relationship had taken a sudden shift.

After they'd eaten, they were more relaxed, though still wary.

'I saw Joyce this afternoon,' Kate proffered.

'Oh yes? How's she?'

'Same as usual. Derek's got a job coming up – receptionist. He wants me to take it.'

'How do you feel about that?'

'Maybe I should. Get me out of the house. It's time I brought some money in.'

'Don't do it for the *money*. We don't need that. He'd only pay peanuts anyway.'

'It'd be something though, wouldn't it? Something of my own. I wouldn't be sponging on you all the time.'

'*Sponging?* That's a funny word to use.'

'It's the right one. I'm a dead weight so far as you're concerned, aren't I?'

'I don't see you as that. Why are you talking like this, Kate?'

'Because I'm fed up with myself. I want to do something.'

He looked at her wonderingly, hearing her speak the words for the second time that day. 'You'll have to decide what you want to do, love. I don't think working for Derek's the answer.'

'Neither do I. He'd probably be pawing me behind a screen, if he has such a thing there.'

'I don't know about that,' Colin said, smiling faintly. 'But I'm sure you can do better than that anyway.'

'Can I? I haven't had a decent job since leaving school. *Tourism!* Jesus.'

'It's how we met, darling.'

'Yes. The only decent thing that came out of it.'

'You seemed to like it at the time.'

'Shows what a good actress I am. Can you imagine what it's like? All those girls think about is shagging and sunshine.'

'Goes for the clientèle too. Present company excepted, of course,' he said lightly.

He regretted the words at once. They sounded false, in the context of their newfound selfconsciousness.

'What do you want to do then? Any idea?' he asked quickly.

'Not a clue. That's the trouble.'

He pondered, sinking into the safety of the subject, still feeling strange to himself, a sense of guilt growing uneasily inside him like a foreign body. With sudden inspiration he said, 'What about an Open University degree?'

'What?' She stared at him as if he were mad.

'You could do it OK.'

'Don't be stupid.'

'I'm not. It'd be just up your street. Studying here, in your own time.'

'With my brain? You've got to be joking.'

'There you go again. Underrating yourself,' he said recklessly.

She looked at him, startled. 'What do you mean?'

'Well, you're always doing that, aren't you? You don't give yourself a chance. You could do it if you tried. You could do it easily.'

'But I don't want to do it. I don't want anything like that.'

'Why not? It would be good for you. You'd be stretching yourself.'

He was excited, snatching words wildly out of the air because they increased his sense of security, building a wall with them between his old self and the new.

'All I want is a simple job. Don't do this to me, Colin.'

He knew he had gone too far, was in danger of alerting her suspicion because of the sheer strangeness of his behaviour.

'All right then,' he said. 'Let's think of something else. There's lots of things you could be doing.'

'Just one would do.'

Yvonne was inside him now, a reality. He tried to push her away, gently.

'Maybe I'll try working in a charity shop,' Kate said.

'Y-e-e-s,' he murmured, only half taking it in. 'That's a good idea.'

'Do you think so?' she asked eagerly.

'Mm. A charity shop . . . yes . . . I think it's a very good idea, Kate. There's one in the village, isn't there?'

'Two.'

'*Two?* I didn't know that.'

'A new one's just opened by the library.'

'Has it? I hadn't noticed.'

She realised his attention was drifting away and snapped, 'You don't notice anything, do you? All you think about is your work.'

'That's not fair, Kate,' he said plaintively.

'Nothing's fair. Haven't you noticed?'

She swept out of the room, clattered the dirty crocks into the dishwashing machine. He sighed, and thought of Yvonne.

She dreamt of her first boyfriend, Martin, that night. They were kissing, but his lips were not those of a fifteen-year-old but of someone much more knowing and dangerous. 'No, Martin,' she protested. 'I have to go home. Please Martin. Please.' His lips grew huge until they covered every part of her and she flailed around, trying to escape. She was shouting but no voice came, she was covered in mucus, she was drowning. She woke up, surprised by the stillness. Colin was sleeping, undisturbed. The reality of Martin still clung to her, she saw his thin adolescent face in every detail. To shake him off she padded barefoot to the bathroom. She did not switch on the light but just stood there, regaining herself. Colin took over, the smell and the shape of him were there in the shaving cream and aftershave she could dimly make out in the semi-darkness. The dream had aroused her, she wanted to wake Colin up and feel him inside her, for she would be the possessor and he the possessed. It was she who had first taken the initiative in their lovemaking, and she felt her power over him to be total. Colin couldn't escape. The dream was twisted about, given some meaning by the sense of sexual power that now filled her. She slipped back into bed and curled her arm around him. He stirred only slightly, for what else could the poor man do? He could not rebel, and would not want to. She drifted away into sleep and when she woke up remembered nothing, neither the dream of Martin nor her sense of mastery over Colin. What she knew, and did not doubt for a moment, was that she would go to the new charity shop and see if they could make use of her.

'I'm sorry, Gwynne. I really am.'

'Are you hell.' Gwynne Tecwyn glowered at her, a tic by his right eye giving the bizarre impression that he was winking at her.

'Yes. Actually I am,' returned Carol coolly. 'I thought we could work together well on this.'

They were sitting quite close to one another, just the two of them in her office; she had deliberately moved from her desk to make the awkward encounter more amenable, a gesture which had so far proved unproductive.

'So why did you bring your *father* into it in the first place?' Gwynne asked, with a sneering emphasis on the word 'father.'

'Obvious,' said Carol, clipped. 'He's got a good track record. He seemed the best man for the job.'

'*Myn uffern.* It's years since he did anything.'

'That doesn't mean he's lost it. *Trapp's Gold* won a Bafta.'

'When was that, for God's sake?'

'I don't know . . . ten years maybe.'

'Ten years!' mocked Gwynne. 'That's a bloody lifetime.' She stared back at him, challenging.

'Francis Kent,' he scoffed. 'Why didn't he call himself Ted Sloane then?'

'He can call himself what he likes, surely? It's up to him.'

Gwynne, his run-to-seed athleticism still making him a powerful figure, jerked forward, making her flinch instinctively.

'I've read those *novels* of his. They were good. He could write in those days.'

She nodded, waiting.

'Why didn't he bring out more then? Why did he give it all up?'

'You must ask him that, not me.'

Gwynne gave her a long look, then sat back, a small smile teasing his full, strangely feminine lips.

'This is the worst case of nepotism I've ever come across,' he said softly. 'It's utterly disgraceful.'

'If you're going to be offensive,' said Carol evenly, 'you can piss off.'

'I intend complaining to the Writers' Guild.'

'You can complain to the man in the moon. It won't do you any good.'

He was looking amused now, the glitter in his eyes compelling her to remember jollier occasions than this.

'I can't believe you're doing this to me, Carol,' he murmured, snake-like. 'You of all people.'

'I've got no choice, Gwynne,' she replied, ignoring the insinuation. 'I've got to get this right.'

'And you really think you will – with him?'

'Yes. I do.'

'But he's too old, for God's sake! And he knows bugger-all about Wales!'

'He knows more than you think.'

He shook his head disbelievingly. 'Well,' he said heavily, 'on your own head be it.'

'Exactly.' She stood up, glad that the sudden weakness in her legs did not betray itself. 'Well, thanks for coming in, Gwynne. I'm grateful for all the work you've put in – you know that.'

'You don't have to give me shit, Carol.' He got to his feet, his stubble, the thickset mass of him, his very nearness, making him, briefly, a figure of menace.

'If this thing bombs, you'll be a laughing-stock – you know that, don't you?'

'I'll take the risk.'

He passed her, too close for comfort, but paused by the door.

'Hope you don't still wear a basque, Carol,' he said. 'It doesn't suit you.'

She blushed deeply at this callous reminder of a one-night stand she preferred to forget. With a glance of malicious triumph, he left.

Ted thrust the spade deep into the clayey soil, turning it over with a sense of acute pleasure. After the overnight rain it stuck together in lumps which he broke up with hefty thwacks of the blade, pausing often for breath. The exertion tired him, but at the same time toned up his muscles so that he knew that later he would feel fitter and younger for it. He paced himself, staring at the minutiae revealed by his turning of the sod: wispy roots of fragile plants, writhing worms, flurries of grey, squirming woodlice. He was about to pack it in after an hour when he struck something hard: a plump lemonade bottle, encrusted and filled with soil, something like a milk bottle in shape, the manufacturer's name standing out in embossed capital letters. He stared at it wonderingly. It took him back more than fifty years, to a terraced house in Cardiff where his grandfather shook his head gravely and said, 'No, lad, I can't let you have them, I'm sorry.'

'Why not? I'll look after them, I promise.'

'I know you will. But I want them meself.' The old man, his Bradford accent strong as ever after thirty years in Wales, smiled to ease the pain of the boy's disappointment. 'You understand, don't you? They remind me of things. The time I could run. Couldn't do that now to save me life.'

Ted, barely ten, had stared, fascinated, at the turn-of-the-century photograph of Gramps standing to attention before a race, in singlet and shorts and with his arms held close to his sides. He had looked impossibly young to the boy, yet still recognisably his grandfather. Beside him in the photo stood his sole opponent in the race, tall and moustachioed and with a proud look in his eyes, as if he couldn't be beaten. But Gramps had shown him all right. He'd been one of the best runners in the world.

'Tell you what, son.' Arthur Sloane leaned over confidentially. 'When I'm past it – really past it – you can have the lot – photos, medals, everything.'

Ted's face glowed. 'Can I, Gramps?'

Arthur nodded. 'I'll tell Auntie Vi. She won't forget.'

The old pop bottle conjured up these images of the past as if it had the power of Aladdin's lamp. After holding it for a few seconds, Ted tossed it onto the rubbish heap that was growing steadily bigger at the bottom of the garden. He clunked his spade onto the ground two or three times, ridding it of the damp earth caking the blade, then put it in the shed before taking off his boots and going indoors. Time to do some writing.

He padded up to the bathroom, washed his hands and face, changed from his gardening clothes and went into his workroom. It overlooked the rear of the cottage, the far side from the river. There was open countryside to the right, but to the left the outer fringes of Hollybush abutted scrubby fields typical of the no-man's-land between town and country. It struck him anew how strange it was that he should be living in Cardiff, a city which, as a boy, had held such glamour for him because of its association with his grandfather. If only Gramps were here now! Yet – another strange thought – he was nearly as old now as Gramps had been then. The twists and turns of a fate that had brought him from Birmingham to the Welsh capital – little more than a hundred miles in geographical distance but oh! so far in terms of experience – engulfed him in a sense of mystery and awe.

But this wouldn't do. He had work to accomplish. He sat at his desk, switched on his Amstrad 9512 word processor, slipped a hard three-inch disk into the drive, pressed C on the keyboard to create a new document and, after a moment's reflection, named it 'Soap.001.' He smiled grimly, and began typing.

8

Tiny rivulets coursing down the french window blurred the image of the neat suburban garden beyond. Plenty of water, but of the wrong kind. Sometimes the ache for a sea view became physical in Joyce Andrews, located somewhere between her bowels and breasts. She did not count the expanse of Bristol Channel visible from the clifftop path at Penarth where they sometimes took the children on a Sunday afternoon; for her that wasn't sea at all, simply a wet greyness with tiny, fretful waves worrying the muddy shore like a spaniel. Sea of a kind began in the Gower Peninsula, forty miles to the west, but for real sea you had to go to the west coast of Wales and Cardigan Bay, where the proud Atlantic rollers provided a dramatic backdrop that put the pusillanimous splashes at Penarth to shame. The yearning for them was stronger some times than others and now, on this wet Monday morning, she had an acute attack of *hiraeth*. How much longer could she stand living in Cardiff? There was much about it that she liked: the shops and Roath Park lake, with its funny lighthouse memorial to Scott of the Antarctic (who had sailed from Cardiff, then a busy port instead of a clapped-out dockland with pretensions to yuppydom), and if she and Derek fancied an evening out there were plenty of restaurants and bars. But she was a Cardi, and the sea was in her blood. Her grandfather had been a seaman, and his father before

66

him, a portrait of the latter, whiskered and heavy with Victorian gravitas, having an honoured place on the wall of the little-used parlour of the big manse in Aberystwyth where she had grown up, the only child of the late Rev. Leo Davies and the highly unlate Clarissa Davies. 'I'm a landlubber,' Leo would declare heartily, loosening his dog collar as he tucked into a Sunday dinner of lamb and mint sauce after morning service in Bethel English Methodist Church. 'Catch me catching crabs in the hungry ocean.' He had spoken little about his own father, and Joyce wondered what hurt lay hidden behind that roguish smile and devil-may-care manner. Not for him the life-denying piety of some of the deacons of Bethel who had looked at him with scarce-concealed disapproval, seeing his levity as unchristian. They had bothered him not at all. 'God gave us laughter,' he would say. 'It's the other fellow has the long faces.'

With the children, Rhian and Owain, safely in school and Derek in his dental surgery, drilling and filling away with the quiet satisfaction of one who has found his true vocation in life, Joyce made the beds, shoved the latest load into the washing-machine and sat down with the *Daily Mail* crossword and a cup of Nescafé. Then, having filled in a few squares, she looked thoughtful and gripped her mug with both hands. Something Brendan had said when he'd popped in with those tickets thrust itself to the front of her attention, tantalising and ambiguous. 'You must come to our Hallowe'en party, Joyce. You'll enjoy it, I'm sure.' The innuendo was obvious: something naughty might be expected. But what? Joyce wondered. Nothing she could get involved in anyway. Derek was far too straight for that. But would she do anything anyway, if the chance arose? A part of her, quite a large part if she were honest, was intrigued by the rumours that went around Hollybush of incredible goings-on in the swinging Sixties. Keyrings thrown on the floor, husband-and-wife swapping, all that. But what did they do with the kids when they were going to bed with the neighbours? And how could they look each other in the face afterwards? She was half inclined to think it was all make-believe, the stuff of urban legend, but all the same she felt a frisson of excitement when she thought of it. Because, let's face it (she said to herself), life was pretty bloody dull, wasn't it? If Brendan and Sophie had found something more exciting in the Sixties, good luck to them.

But what *was* this Hallowe'en party he had hinted at? She'd have to find out. And if Derek didn't want anything to do with it, she'd go on her bloody own.

'No, Chris,' Yvonne Morris said firmly. 'I'm sorry. I can't.' The voice on the end of the line became more peevish, causing her to make small gestures of exasperation, visible only to herself. Her self-control, stretched to the limit, suddenly snapped and she said clearly, 'For Christ's sake, give over.'

A brief silence, into which her interlocuter's amazement seeped like a trickle through a dam wall, was followed by a stunned, 'What was that?'

'I'm tired of your bleating. Why don't you give it a rest?'

Peevishness turned to outrage. Yvonne ended the monologue by hanging up. Then, with a faint smile, she took the pale blue receiver from its cradle and laid it face up on the coffee table, like a small creature gasping for air.

She imagined him in the converted bedroom he called his 'office' in Swansea, stamping around in futile rage before trying her number again. She would not be there. It was unusual for her to have a Monday off and she would make the most of it. Listening to her boyfriend's – or what would now be her ex-boyfriend's – protests was definitely not part of the deal. She had a present to buy for her mother's birthday, and she would take her time about choosing it.

She inspected herself critically in the full-length mirror she had placed beside the dark, looming sideboard. She did not like her appearance: it was too heavy by far, like the sideboard and the rest of the furniture in this rented flat. It would do for now, but one day she'd need to get her own place. But, she reflected gloomily, she couldn't do much about that gypsyish skin of hers – where the hell had it come from? – and the sooty, bushy eyebrows that looked like the thatch from a burnt-out cottage. What was the answer, plastic surgery? Impatiently she glanced through the window; the early-morning rain seemed to be easing off. After a moment's hesitation, she put the phone back on its cradle, switched on the ansaphone and hurried out before the damned thing started ringing again.

It was a short, brisk walk to the shops in Wellfield Road, where she could happily spend hours just browsing. 'I *love* this street!' she had heard a woman exclaim there once, and she shared the sentiment. There were shops of all kinds, selling books and health foods and antiques and jewellery and heaven knows what altogether. It was in an old, solid part of Cardiff, the district of Roath that had grown in pace with the port in Victorian times and was now pretty sure of itself, although a bit run down at the edges. There was nothing like this in Swansea any more: Hitler's bombs had kicked the guts out of the old town, and the rebuilt centre still looked like something run up out of plastic and plywood for a fourth-rate film set.

Her mother. What should she get her? Clothes were out of the question: whatever she bought, it wouldn't be right. 'It's very kind of you, darling, but . . .' How well she knew that 'darling, but'! Yvonne was half inclined to think that on the day Mum had given birth, she had given her a disappointed look and murmured, 'Yes, darling, but . . .' She sighed inwardly. She loved her mother, and yet . . .

She took her time, shopped a little for herself, went to the café opposite the bank for a mid-morning coffee, and could not stop her thoughts sliding in a forbidden direction. . .

Did he fancy her? There were signs that he might, and yet . . . What should she do about it if he did? Was she ready for an affair? The very thought made her head hot, her stomach feel like it had the day Mum had found out about her and Julian Reynolds. God! What was wrong with her? She wasn't a baby. She was twenty-six, and could do what she liked! The fact that Colin was married didn't worry her a bit. It was just that he was so nice, she was afraid that if she had him once, she wouldn't want to let him go.

That bitch of a wife of his . . . she knew she was a bitch, even though she'd never met her. The way Colin kow-towed to her . . . the way he *worried* about her. And there was nothing wrong with her! She knew it! It was Kate this and Kate that . . . and Kate didn't seem to do anything. It wasn't as if she had kids as an excuse. She was just plain idle.

Impatient with herself, not for the first time that morning, Yvonne skimmed through her *Independent* as she sipped her coffee, her slim fingers – more elegant than she ever imagined them to be – turning the pages lightly. They caught the attention of an elderly man sitting alone with his *Guardian* and his memories. She glanced up, saw him staring, finished her coffee quickly and left.

The old man did not feel foolish, but regretful. Inside himself, he was as young as she was.

She returned to the jeweller's where she'd done some window-shopping earlier, and decided on a supposedly 'Celtic-style' bracelet for her mother. Back in her flat, she found there was a message on her ansaphone. Bloody Chris again! She jabbed the button impatiently. But it was Colin, checking on something that was not at all urgent. Returning his call, she could not keep a slightly breathy tone out of her voice, and did not try.

'Of course, dear. We can do with all the help we can get.'

Jill Gosport, fiftyish, motherly, smiled indulgently at the woman who had come to the shop offering her services. She knew her by sight, and had always thought she had an edgy look about her. It was there now, in her bright – too bright – eyes and upfront manner which, to Jill's way of thinking, suggested something forced and unnatural. If she'd been asked to define her misgivings she would have said that here was a woman putting on an act, but not in an unpleasant way. *It's all nerves* – the phrase passed through her mind barely consciously, like a slight breeze lifting the corners of a newspaper, as she blandly outlined the tasks that Kate would have to perform.

'Of course, you won't be paid anything. You know that, don't you, dear?' said Jill with a smile, remembering the 'volunteer' who had abruptly brought the conversation to an end by declaring that naturally, as a self-employed person, she would expect her wages to be paid without tax deducted at source.

'Naturally,' replied Kate shortly. 'I wouldn't expect to be paid.'

'Well, that's all right then, isn't it?' said Jill comfortably. 'Now, what did you say your name was?'

'Kate. Kate Dawson.'

'Good. Shall I call you Kate? We're all on first-name terms here. I'm Jill, and that's Pam.' She nodded at a thin, dark-haired woman hanging frocks up on a display unit. Pam and Kate exchanged wary smiles as Jill continued, 'Have you had any experience of shop work, dear? You know we have to be terribly tactful and polite.' She trilled a laugh unexpectedly, the sound appearing too shrill for the ample body.

Kate briefly explained that she had been a tourist rep abroad, which impressed Jill considerably.

'My dear! You'll find us awfully boring after that. But you must tell us all about it some time. It sounds frightfully exciting.'

'Not really -' began Kate, but Jill would have none of it, launching into a recollection of a divine holiday she and Terry had spent on the Algarve at a delicious little resort which had been utterly spoilt since by the onslaught of Lego-like hotels and lager-fuelled tourists. Kate and Pam again exchanged swift glances, this time slightly more sympathetic.

'Now, how often do you think you'd like to come in, Kate?' Jill asked eventually.

'Oh – a couple of times a week, possibly.'

'Would that be half days or full days?'

'Half days at first, I think. Until I get used to it,' she added, at the hint of a frown.

'Well, dear, you must please yourself, of course. But I do think you ought to give yourself a *proper* chance.' Jill's smile returned, maternal and understanding. 'I hope you'll find us all *very* good company. Not that there's many of us yet. This is all very new, isn't it, Pam?'

Pam nodded, gave Kate a more appraising glance, appeared to like what she saw.

'Now, there's just some formalities we have to go through, if you'd like to come through to the office for a moment. Nothing to worry about at all. Just some personal details for our records.' A reassuring smile from Jill, and Kate followed her to the inevitable computer.

Outside the charity shop again, Kate took a deep breath. She'd actually done it! She hadn't thought she would, when it came to the crunch. It was a start, a definite start. After the initial triumph, her knees felt a bit wobbly. It was a quarter to four. She slipped into a twee little café with chintzy curtains, and ordered a cappucino and a Danish pastry.

9

It was impossible to drift into Clwb Ddraig Goch – the Red Dragon Club – by accident. To reach it one went down a tight alleyway and turned into what had been one of Cardiff's most notorious 'courts' in Victorian times, a smelly, rat-infested slum where half-starved children clad in dirty smocks or shirts stared at the occasional visiting photographer with blank incomprehension. The prints resulting from these daring excursions by the middle classes now appeared from time to time in exhibitions clobbered together by socially-conscious librarians and educationists, but the children who stared out of the frame were blissfully unaware of being stared back at, so much later. The slums, like the kids, were long gone, their places taken by early 20th century buildings which had been stripped down, done up and rehashed many times over. The area once occupied by four hovels in Gassners Court was now covered by a mock-Gothic excrescence which had been, in its time, private school for young ladies, bakery and confectionery store, lawyer's offices and Welsh HQ of a trade union. After standing empty for a year or two, it now offered counselling on its first floor, high-interest loans masquerading as financial advice on the ground floor and Clwb Ddraig Goch in the basement, a haven for Welsh speakers in the heart of the nation's overwhelmingly English-speaking capital.

Early on this Monday evening the club had a listless air, its few occupants still hung over from the weekend or brooding over the pointlessness of beginning yet another week in the same boring old job. Even the Welsh flag hanging from the wall opposite the bar seemed dispirited, reflecting a malaise springing not from yet another national rugby defeat but the condition of life itself. The jauntiness of the posters urging the clientèle to support patriotic causes was curiously at odds with the atmosphere, and the taped rock thundered unheeded.

Gwynne Tecwyn, black-leather-jacketed, morose, scowled into his Stella. 'I'll get the bastard bitch,' he mouthed, 'if it's the last thing I fucking do.'

The young woman sitting opposite placidly turned a page of *Hello!* and with slim, elegant fingers took a cigarette from the packet she had left open on the table.

'It's so unprofessional,' he protested. 'Who else would employ their fucking father, for Godsake?'

Ffion Tomos feigned complete absorption in the exclusive coverage of a celeb wedding in Surrey.

'If I told *Wales on Sunday* half I know about her, she'd be finished.'

Ffion's continued silence suddenly got to him. 'Well, say something,' he said irritably.

She gave him a long look, her light hazel eyes cool and appraising. 'What do you expect me to say?'

'Well, don't you think it's bloody disgusting?'

Her shoulders twitched with the slightest hint of a shrug. 'What's there to stop her, if she wants to?'

Gwynne glared at her. 'Nepotism!' he cried. 'It's the curse of Wales. Half the people at the BBC are up each other's arses.'

She flicked a flame from her silver lighter. 'Incest and buggery combined, that it?'

Her poised, elegant manner, so perfectly complementing her dark business suit, roused something evil in Gwynne. 'You look like the Queen of the fucking May,' he said.

'You look like a lump of shit,' she returned equably.

Instead of infuriating him further, her words had a strangely calming effect. 'But don't you think it's bad?' he pleaded. 'It's knocked me sideways, I can tell you.'

'I can understand that,' said Ffion, more sympathetically. 'But there's not a lot you can do about it, is there?'

'I can complain to the Writers' Guild.'

'Y-e-e-es,' she conceded. 'But what will they tell you? She hasn't broken any laws, has she?'

'Unwritten ones,' said Gwynne stoutly.

Ffion's shrug, this time, was more emphatic. 'That doesn't mean anything, does it? She can contract anyone she likes. She'd have checked it out with her MD, presumably.'

'Oh yes,' Gwynne said sarcastically. 'She'll have done that all right. She knows how to cover her back.'

'Well then.'

Taking a long swig of his pint, Gwynne became uncomfortably aware of the stare she was directing at him. Before she spoke, he already knew he had said more than was good for him.

'Why do you think *Wales on Sunday* would be interested in her? What's she done?' she asked curiously.

'Well, you know what people in this game are like,' he blustered. 'They've all got something to hide.'

'Yes,' she persisted, 'but what in particular?'

He was unusually silent.

'You've been shagging her, have you?' Ffion asked evenly.

'Fuck no! I wouldn't touch her with a barge pole.'

Ffion's amused, come-off-it look brought an unaccustomed flush to Gwynne's face.

'Well, that's all right then, isn't it?' she observed. 'You're quits.'

'What do you mean, quits?'

'Well, you screwed her and now she's screwing you.'

Gwynne did his best to look offended. 'That's a pretty outrageous thing to say, if you don't mind me saying so.'

Ffion smiled. 'Was she worth it?' she asked in a laid-back, tantalising way. 'It's costing you, isn't it, now she's ditched you.'

'That's not why she did it!' he said hotly.

'Oh, why then? I thought that's what you were suggesting. It can't be because you weren't delivering the goods, could it?'

'You bitch,' breathed Gwynne.

'Thank you very much,' replied Ffion gracefully.

Gwynne glared at her and carried his pint to the one-armed bandit in a gloomy distant corner. She stayed where she was, a thoughtful look on her pale, sculpted face. After a while she sauntered across to where he stood, sullenly feeding the machine far more coins than it spewed back.

'Of course,' she murmured, 'you could try the more subtle approach.'

He maintained a brief, proud silence for some seconds. 'If you've got something to say, Ffion, fucking say it,' he said sullenly.

'Charming,' she said. 'Up yours, big boy.' She turned away.

'No – wait!'

She paused, smiling.

'What've you got in mind then?' he asked reluctantly.

'Interested now, are you?'

He stared at her lovely, teasing face, itching to lay hands on those perfect breasts, so tantalisingly close.

'If you're ready,' she said sinuously, 'we might talk about it.'

He gave the handle of the machine a last, brutal tug, watched the gaudy symbols spin unrelentingly and then, with a jerk of the head, walked upstairs and out of the club with her.

10

Sir Charles Lewis idly turned the pages of one of the professional journals that were regularly delivered to the office. He was in no mood for work on this late Monday afternoon; had been feeling restless all day. The big word, 'retirement', loomed ever larger in his thoughts. He'd be sixty-three next birthday; why was he carrying on working? He could sell the business tomorrow; there'd been offers enough. Until recently, there'd been no need to pose the question; he'd still been happy in his work, happily busy, the move to Cardiff Bay from the city centre successfully completed, a bright outlook for the partnership assured.

The partnership . . . that was a joke. Charles Lewis, George Taylor, David Webb . . . the words before him blurred, became overlaid by a mental picture of how they had all been thirty years ago, the brightest young architects in Cardiff, helping to shape the new Wales with their clean-cut modern buildings. They'd been up for it then all right, snatching commissions from under the noses of the old fuddy-duddies still stuck in the mindset of the thirties. And they'd had some fun, too right they had . . . the scarlet tip of his nose twitched as he soaked himself in joyful memories . . . But now Dave was dead, and George only looked in once in a blue moon, and it was all left to him, the senior partner still keeping the show on the road. And for what? He sighed. He'd just about had enough of it.

The words on the glossy page came back into focus. What was this? 'How stress-free is your space?' some prat was asking in bold italics. 'We look at the impact of the new feminised office.' *Feminised office!* God, the garbage these people wrote.

He tossed the journal aside. So *would* he pack it all in? Could he bring himself to sell the practice? If so, who to? That cocky young lot he kept bumping into at the County Club? They gave him a guts-ache, but they knew what they were up to all right. Had made a good job of that new leisure centre up the Valleys. Had the wherewithal too. He'd screw the bastards for all he could get. Celia would be pleased. She'd been nagging him to retire for years. And yet, and yet . . . He still got a buzz from it. Up to a point. But the point was getting lower every time. Maybe he would, maybe he wouldn't. But if he did, what would happen to his staff?

Oh, bugger the bloody staff. They could look after themselves. And there weren't many now – only eleven on the payroll. Against thirty-five at one time. Technology, change. All was change and decay. Only eleven! And barely one of those he really cared about. Well, maybe two . . . Colin certainly, Yvonne perhaps. They made a good match. The idea, taking him unawares, startled him. Maybe they ought to be – how did they put it these days – an *item*? No, no, it wouldn't do, it wouldn't do in the least . . . but wouldn't it be one in the eye for Kate – he was quite convinced she was always looking down her nose at him – oh, wouldn't it just! Colin and Yvonne . . . yes . . . A mischievous smile crinkled the corners of his thin, careful lips. Perhaps . . . when the time was ripe . . . a tiny, quite undetectable push in the right direction . . . what possible harm could it do? . . . Hm?

'But that's marvellous!' enthused Colin. 'When do you start?'

'They left it to me,' replied Kate. 'I might go in tomorrow.'

'What were they like about it then? OK, were they?'

'They were fine,' she said irritably. 'Why shouldn't they be?'

'No reason, darling. Just asking.'

'I haven't got two heads, you know.'

'Haven't you?' he said buoyantly, then, seeing her expression: 'Sorry.' Resentment followed swiftly on the heels of remorse: why was she so bloody hard on him? 'I'm going for a shower,' he said, and ran upstairs out of her way. Throwing his clothes off in the bathroom, he felt free and uninhibited. He had to watch his words so carefully these days! And all he wanted to do was help!

The shower cubicle completed his sense of being separate from everyone, untouchable. He remembered, with a thrill of exquisite guilt, how he had phoned Yvonne at home that day. It had taken a bit of doing; he'd had to steel himself to do it. He'd broken an unwritten law of the practice: one only rang colleagues at home in emergency. But she hadn't seemed to mind a bit, had obviously been glad to talk to him. He recalled the breathiness in her voice, a sure sign of interest in him. But now he would have to follow it up or lose face with her; and for a few seconds he felt the slightest sense of foreboding. 'Rubbish!' he cried out loud, to the gel and the shower curtains, soaping himself more vigorously, as if to dispel the thick crawl of guilt across his scalp.

He had always been attracted to her, ever since she had arrived to take over the admin. work previously done by that horse-faced old biddy, Ethel Jones, who'd been with the firm since the year dot. At first (he recalled now with amusement) he had wondered if she'd be up to it; Ethel had conveyed the impression that the job was so onerous, they were lucky to have it performed by only one pair of hands. But Yvonne had made light of it, convincing even Charlie – who'd had more than a soft spot for Ethel – that the older woman had deliberately made hard work of it all. Yvonne was efficient, intelligent, good with clients and computer literate, which was something Ethel would never have been in a million years. What's more she was sexy; not heavily so but in a subtle, understated way. And he'd had the feeling, for a long time, that she fancied him a little.

As he dried himself, he did his best to damp down his sense of elation and anticipation. His marriage was still all-important; all he wanted from Yvonne, he assured himself, was friendship. Friendship laced, perhaps, with the lightest frisson of romance? He shrugged the thought away, and went downstairs feeling cool and refreshed.

He managed to hit the right note with Kate, over the pasta she'd cooked to near perfection.

'So what's the set-up at this charity shop then?' he asked. 'Who's in charge?'

'Do you really want to know?' returned Kate, not quite mollified.

'Of course I do. Why not?'

'You wanted me to do the Open University.'

'Well?'

'Well . . . I thought you might think I was copping out.'

He stared at her as if at a stranger. 'Don't be silly. What makes you think that?'

She shrugged. 'I'm not quite sure where we are with each other these days.'

'We're where we've always been, Kate,' he said earnestly. 'Look – I'm glad about this job. Really glad.'

'Are you?'

'Of course.'

Her eyes glistened. She needed his approval, especially now, surrounded as she was with a vague sense of threat for which she could find no definable reason.

'I think it will do you good,' he enthused. 'Really, Kate. Believe me. It's the best thing you've done for years.'

'Do you think so?' she asked eagerly, wanting to believe him.

'Yes, I do.'

Feeling absurdly proud of herself, and grateful to him, she leaned over the table and kissed him. He was surprised, and then pleased, until a sense of shame seeped through him, poisoning the moment.

Although she frequently complained about the children, Joyce Andrews enjoyed being a mother, and one of the things she enjoyed most was meeting the children from school. She called them both little hellers, but actually only the elder of the two, eight-year-old Rhian, was difficult: sturdy, in-your-face, she was a proper handful. Owain, two years younger, took after his father: shy, pale, sandy-haired, he was bullied a little by his sister and needed to stand up for himself more. Owain came out of school first, from the infants' department of Ysgol Owain Glyndŵr, to be followed a little later by Rhian from the juniors, always full of herself and of what she was doing. While she waited for them, Joyce chatted to the other mums, not always in Welsh because quite a lot of them spoke only English, giving their offspring the benefit of a Welsh-medium education because they thought it would provide more individual attention than the 'normal' state school. It was their way of getting a quasi-private education for their children without the boring necessity of paying for it (although, heaven forbid, they would never have admitted this); and of course, bilingualism was an asset in the new Wales, wasn't it?

Although she worked part-time as a physiotherapist, Joyce met the kids from school at least four times a week. When she couldn't get there her mother-in-law obliged, and although Evelyn was as good as gold in many ways, Joyce did not like her doing too much with the kids. She was English for a start, from Evesham, and although Joyce would have strenuously denied being racist in any way, there was something about that soft, russet-apple intonation that grated on her. Moreover she was the daughter of a milkman, and Joyce, as the product of an Aberystwyth manse, had a snobbish sense of superiority, albeit unadmitted, over anyone from a working-class background. (She felt superior to her father-in-law too, but for different reasons: George Andrews, a retired bank manager, was a typical Cardiffian with a TV aerial turned to Bristol and the gall to suggest that her children would be disadvantaged by having Welsh 'thrust down their throats'.)

There was much that the waiting mums found to talk about that day, with the autumn half-term coming up and the first intimation that the school might be doing something rather special for Christmas, and Joyce was chatting away quite happily when she suddenly became aware of an unfamiliar figure standing alone: Brendan, no less, the silvery-haired relic of the Swinging Sixties who carried around the faint aura of decadence that she found so appealing. As soon as she could free herself from the matriarchal cluster, Joyce approached him in her brightest young-mum manner. 'Brendan! What on earth are you doing here?'

'Meeting Jonathan – our grandson,' he jovially replied. 'No law against it, is there?'

'No, but – I didn't know you had *grandchildren,* Brendan?'

'Didn't you? Shows how much you know me then, doesn't it? We've got two – Jonathan and Emily. You've seen us with them, haven't you?'

'No, I haven't. You surprise me, Brendan. I've never seen you as the grandfatherly sort.'

'Think I'm too young for that, do you?' he said archly. 'Well, I can't say I blame you.' He gave vent to his famously rich laugh, the merriment of an old dog who just won't lie down.

'Where's your wife – she here too?'

'No, Sophie's at the dentist – though not Derek's, I'm afraid,' he apologised swiftly. 'She sees a right old jaw-breaker. Been going there for years.'

'Shame on her! How old's Jonathan then?'

'Ten. Going up to Cardiff High next year.'

'Oh? Not to Ysgol Gyfun Aneurin?' enquired Joyce, eyebrows raised.

'No – their mother thinks enough is enough,' replied Brendan mysteriously. 'Oh, by the way,' he added as the first infants to emerge began pelting down the path under the trees towards the school gate. 'You *are* coming to our party next week, aren't you?'

'The Hallowe'en do? Of course. Wouldn't miss it for anything. What time d'you want us there?'

'Oh, eightish. Whenever you like, really.'

'Right. Do we need to dress up for it?'

'If you like. Or dress down,' he leered. 'Oh, by the way – there *is* something different about it – did I tell you?'

'No? What's that?' asked Joyce curiously, with a sudden, grotesque vision of keyrings being thrown down and people shuffling upstairs in various permutations of partners.

'Well, we're asking everyone to invite a surprise guest along – someone they may not know very well. Adds a bit of spice, you know? The thrill of the unexpected. I know you'll like that.' His eyes twinkled abominably.

'You wicked old thing. That might be asking for trouble.'

'Hope so, or there's no point in it, is there? Oh, here's your lad – hullo, son! Or should I say *shoo-my?*'

Owain gave him a cautious glance. 'Mr Collins,' Joyce reminded him. 'We don't see him here very often, do we?'

Owain looked away, saying nothing, instinctively disliking Brendan.

'Tell me, Joyce, do you think your next-door neighbours would like an invite?' Brendan asked casually.

'They might. Give them a ring. You know their number, don't you?'

'No, I don't. But I'll find them in the book, I expect.' He was looking oddly at Joyce. 'Strange sort of girl, isn't she, Colin's wife?'

'Kate? She's OK – when you get to know her.'

'That's what I mean. Getting to know her's the thing – I imagine. Ah well. Here's the boy. Bit sooner than I expected. Be seeing you then.'

'Yes. 'Bye, Brendan.'

11

The vague sense of threat that she had felt earlier enveloped Kate in the night like a shroud. She woke up fighting for breath, with a sense of rising panic. She wrenched herself up in bed, fists pressed down tight against the mattress. She couldn't go through with it, she couldn't! The two women she had met, Jill and Pam, had become figures of nightmare in her imagination, their every word and gesture distorted in memory. Jill's motherly supplications, her 'do-come-and-join-us' charm, were now a loathsome attempt to entice her into a trap, while Pam's cool detachment breathed a hostility which betokened only persecution of the meanest kind. Why had she agreed to do it? What right had Colin to force her? Her heart, palpitating wildly, was doing its best to leap out of her body. She willed it to steady itself, breathing deeply, each intake and exhalation a long, deliberate effort, and as her heartbeat slowed and the panic subsided, Colin's steady breathing at her side, his total unawareness of her struggle, became an outrage against her very existence. How *dare* he sleep on like this? How *dare* he talk to her as he had, not realising in the least the immensity of her decision. It was all very well for him, with his male, masterful superiority! He hadn't known what she had known, the sense of worthlessness that still overpowered her! And what was he up to all day, she'd like to know? There'd been something about him lately, something she couldn't put her finger on . . .

Sweat-soaked, exhausted, she drooped into sleep, a calm, soothing sleep that sucked up the last dark shiverings of panic. She was dimly aware, but only as one is aware in a dream, of Colin getting dressed, moving about downstairs, leaving the house quietly. And then the car coughing into life, sidling up the drive and away with sly, male, pantherish invincibility! She seeped back to full consciousness, slowly, in her own time, and it dawned on her with awful certainty that the root of her problems was Colin's physical presence. Free of it she felt cleansed, more whole, in tune with her whole being. She pondered this awesome truth, the day ahead, *her* day, stretching out invitingly for her to do as she would with it.

Her inward eyes focused on a man whom she had admired from afar for almost as long as she could remember, a man who, amazingly, was living only a short distance away. Thinking of him now, she felt a thrill of anticipation that made her throw back the blankets and hurry into the shower, the alone-ness of herself in the husbandless house filling her with a joy she could scarcely contain.

This script! This bloody script! The first two episodes were written – or rather rewritten – and there had been that sudden whoosh! the rush of adrenalin that told him they were fine, the dialogue and story were working. He'd heard the lines in his head and keyed them in, faithfully recording them as if they – his invented characters – were the human reality and he simply the medium they spoke through. This was the joy of all playwriting and when it was not so, when he consciously had to hack out the dialogue, the words lay dead on the page. Oh yes, it was working.

And yet, and yet . . . Something more was needed, a character who could inject the unpredictable into the drama, turning it in unexpected ways as it developed. From episode ten possibly. Or twelve – six weeks into the twice-weekly drama he refused to think of as a soap, because soaps were endless and this one would finish at episode twenty-six.

Ted Sloane switched off the faithful old Amstrad (for so he thought of it, the 'faithful old' cliché fitting his assessment of the machine he refused to swap for a full-blooded, Internet-capable computer), and stretched himself. He stood for a moment, undecided, then went downstairs and into the front garden.

He sensed her approach before he actually saw her. The thrill of creation ran through him, setting him outside himself, the observer of a scene in which he stood watching the young woman advance along the lane towards the cottage. Her step was brisk and something about her – her quick, bold way of walking, the sheer sexuality of her – made him catch his breath. There was still time to turn and go back inside, to the safety of rooms inhabited only by himself and his dog, to a project that would work well enough without that kick a new character would provide. She had not seen him yet, but in a second or two she would. And it would be too late then, ah! too late.

He stood still, resigning himself to his destiny.

Kate was taken by surprise. Her step faltered. Then she strode on along the lane, feigning unawareness of him until they were too close to each other for pretence.

'Taking the air then?' he said pleasantly.

'Yes. Like you.'

'Too nice to stay indoors, isn't it?'

'It is that.'

She had stopped by the gate, smiling up at him as he stood in the sloping garden.

'I've been thinking of what you were saying . . . the last time I saw you,' he went on, a lot more casually than he felt. 'You know . . . about you nearly buying this house. It's made me feel sort of . . . guilty.'

'Guilty?' She stood perplexed, amazed that he had spoken to her at all. 'Why guilty?'

'Well, you wanted it, didn't you? You should be living here, not me.'

She gave a shy half-laugh. 'Don't be silly. We couldn't afford it – I told you. It would have cost too much to put right.'

'Yes, but all the same . . .' There was something boyish about him now; her heart warmed to him. 'Look – would you like to look around the place? You'd be very welcome. See what I've done. Bring your husband if you like. Unless you'd like to come in now – I'll make us a coffee. How's that?' He smiled luminously.

'I don't know,' she said uncertainly; things were happening much too quickly.

'I don't bite, you know – nor does Trinder. But if you don't care to – I shouldn't have asked, I suppose. I'm sorry.' He bent to pick up a large stone – threw it into the heap in the corner.

'You're Ted Sloane, aren't you?' she said carefully.

'Yes – how d'you know?'

She couldn't read his expression. 'I saw it in the *Voice.*'

'Oh, that.' He shrugged. 'I don't know how they found out – nothing to do with me, I assure you.'

'No. I could tell.' She flushed, remembering how snide the piece had been. 'I've read all your books,' she said impetuously. 'They're great.'

He grimaced. 'Written a long time ago, I'm afraid.'

'It doesn't matter. They're still good. When are you going to write some more?'

'Never.'

'Never! Never's a long time.'

'Exactly.' Their conversation hung by a thread. He knew she was about to move on. 'Would you like a copy – signed, I mean?'

'*Would* I?' she said, hardly believing it.

'I've got one or two left – I'd like you to have one.'

'I'd love one. Are you sure?'

'Positive. Come on in.'

He held open the gate and she passed through. Trinder bustled out of the front door, wagging his tail and snuffling into her.

'Down, Trinder! Bad boy!'

'He's all right – really,' she assured him, kneading the dog's neck affectionately. 'I used to have a dog when I was little – not as big as this one though.'

'I can imagine. Where were you living then?'

'In Ireland – Cork. Do you know it?'

'I'm afraid not. Do come in.'

She found herself in a long room, with black-painted beams in the ceiling, a wood-burning stove, a slate mantelpiece with spotty china dogs at either end, a miner's lamp in an alcove and rows of bookshelves against the walls. It had an air of tranquillity, of modish old-worldness mixed with modern utility.

'*Oh!*' she cried, just restraining herself from clapping her hands with delight.

'You like it?' he asked modestly.

'Like it? It's – *wonderful.*'

'Thank you.'

'I never imagined. I mean – I didn't know what to expect. But this – oh, Ted – I can call you Ted, can't I?'

'Of course.'

'This is just right – we'd never have thought of all this. I'm glad you've got it – really. It must be great for your writing.'

He smiled self-deprecatingly. 'Depends what I'm writing, doesn't it? Look, do sit down and make yourself comfortable. You'd like a coffee, would you? Black, white?'

'White please. No sugar.'

He nodded. 'Oh – what do I call you, by the way?'

'Kate. I'm Kate Dawson.'

'Well, just sit down and I'll be back in a tick.'

She sat down and Trinder squatted on the floor by her. She idly squeezed his neck as she looked around with a feeling of amazement. She was inside the cottage, *her* cottage – with *him.* Now she knew that miracles really did happen.

Gwynne Tecwyn was always surprised by how cool and self-possessed Ffion Tomos looked, even when stark naked. Sitting up in bed, she looked absurdly chaste, like Eve before the Fall. All she needed was an unbitten apple in her hands, innocently proffered without a serpent in sight, to complete the picture. It was hard to reconcile the purity of this image with the memory of the woman she had been half an hour before, scratching his thighs lustfully as he tunnelled deep into her honeyed, incomparable body.

'You're a woman and a half all right,' he said admiringly. 'Where the hell do you get these ideas?'

'Same place as the monkey gets its nuts, sunshine,' she replied phlegmatically.

'But . . . will he wear it? I mean, will he do it?'

'Who? Jasper Taylor or Rupert?'

'Both.'

'Don't see why not. Jasper's always out to screw up the Welsh and Rupert's desperate to get on telly.'

'He got a right old pasting last time though, didn't he – Rupert?' said Gwynne pensively, recalling the First Minister of the Welsh Assembly's mauling by the snide, disdainful presenter of the BBC's *Taylor Tonight*.

'No. Time before. Last time he put one over on him.'

'Ah yes. I remember now. Bloody good job too.' Gwynne frowned. 'But do we want to see Rupert duffed up by that snobby English git?'

She shrugged. 'Please yourself. Depends what you want most, doesn't it? Revenge or keeping Rupert out of trouble? Personally, I think they're both equally shitty.'

'Yes, but I prefer a Welsh shit to an English one.'

'There you are then. That's your answer. Forget it.' Ffion, with a quick shake of her hair, swung her long legs over the side of the bed. Her lean white back, the spine shading exquisitely down to the cleft at the top of her bum, tantalisingly faced him. He touched the cleft and she wriggled away, then stood up.

'It's down to you in the end, isn't it, Gwynne? But it'd be nice to see Rupert wriggle. And you'd make things a bit awkward for the lady.'

'And her bloody father. *Bastard*,' said Gwynne viciously. He flung off the bedclothes and pulled on a pair of black boxer shorts neatly embellished, either side of the crotch, with a tiny Welsh dragon motif. 'Right,' he said firmly. 'We'll do it. We'll fucking do it.' He gave a quick, distracted glance at the still naked Ffion. 'But will Jasper really play ball, do you think? Who's going to set the thing up, for Chrissake?'

Ffion smiled, tapped the side of her nose with an elegant forefinger, and said mysteriously, 'Leave it to me, boy *bach*. Just leave it to Ffion.'

'So you see,' Ted said, stretching his legs out. 'That's what I do now.'

'And do you like it?' asked Kate brightly.

'Yes, very much,' he answered confidently; having worked with actors so long, he knew how to put on a bit of a show.

'It must be exciting, working in TV.'

'Well, it has its moments.' The irony was lost on her.

She frowned, wanting to say something full of insight. 'But just writing dialogue is very different from novels, isn't it? You're so good at descriptions in your books – don't you find it a little – frustrating?'

He gave her a keen look. 'It's a different process. You *know* you have to say everything through your characters – so you do it. You just get on with it.' He knew this sounded inadequate so added carelessly, 'Anyway, if my novels work at all – and I don't say they do – it's through the things that people say and do – I don't think I'm so hot on description myself.'

'Oh, but you *are*. And how can you say they don't

work – they're brilliant. God, I wish you'd write another! You'd knock spots off anyone writing now.'

He shook his head. 'No chance of that, I'm afraid. I've got nothing to say.'

'But have you tried? I'm sure you could if –'

'What would be the point of it, Kate? No-one remembers me – I'm a has-been!' he cried passionately, sincerity filling out his voice like a sudden wind in the sails of a near-becalmed boat.

'That's not true! You're famous, Ted – no, don't shake your head. Lots of people remember you – *I* do.'

'God knows why. How did you come across my books, anyway? They don't even put them on the library shelves these days.'

'I *bought* one. Long ago.' Just in time, she stopped herself saying it was on a second-hand bookstall. 'Then I read the rest. Anyway, they *are* in the libraries, you know – if you know where to look.'

'Yes – in the rubbish dump they call Stacks. The nearest thing to a living death for a writer.'

'I've got all your novels at home. I read them over and over.'

'Can't you think of anything else to do?' he asked, the false note entering his voice again.

'I love them,' she said simply. 'They're alive.'

He gave her a long, thoughtful look. 'Thank you,' he said quietly.

Suddenly self-conscious with each other, they fell silent.

'Let's have something stronger,' he said, putting his empty cup down. 'You do drink, I take it?'

'Yes, but – not at this time of day usually.'

'Well,' he said queerly, 'this is an exception, isn't it? What would you like – G and T, wine?'

'Have you got a white wine?'

'Of course. Chardonnay suit you?'

'Perfect.'

He left the room. Kate looked around, hardly able to comprehend what was happening. She was facing one of the windows she used to look at from the river bridge – only now she was inside, looking out. She felt like Alice in Wonderland in the burrow, falling, falling, she knew not where.

He came back with the glass, his fingers extended as he gave it her, so that they might not touch.

He sat opposite her again, a Chilean red in his hand, in an old armchair with high ribbed back and stout, scratched legs.

'Tell me about yourself,' he said, settling himself. 'You're married, of course. What's he do?'

'There's no of course about it,' she said, with a slow smile. 'But he's an architect.'

'An architect,' he repeated, surprised. 'And he didn't want to do this place up for you?'

She shook her head. 'He didn't think it worth it.'

'Oh. I see,' he remarked, unconvincingly. 'And you accepted that?'

'I didn't have much choice.'

'How very quaint. And old-fashioned.'

'Maybe we are – old-fashioned.'

They exchanged a long, searching look.

'What's his name then?' asked Ted at last.

'Colin.'

'Has he got his own firm?'

'No. He works down Cardiff Bay.'

'The Docks. H'm. Does he like it there?'

'He seems to. It's very – modern.'

'I can imagine,' he said dryly. 'So – if you forgive my asking – what do you do with yourself?'

'Nothing.'

'You don't have a job?'

'No.'

'That's why you can sit here – drinking with strange men.'

'I didn't think you were plural.'

'I'm sorry. That was very impudent.'

'It was a bit. I'll go if it offends you.'

'Please. I said I'm sorry.'

She looked down. 'I know it's pathetic. But I haven't been too well lately.'

'I'm sorry. Please forgive me.'

'There's nothing I'd like more,' she lied. 'In fact I'm starting work soon – I had an interview yesterday.'

'You did! That's fine. Who was it with?'

'The charity shop in the village – the new one.'

'I know it. They've got those neat water colours in the window.'

'Have they? I didn't notice.'

'So when do you start there?'

'Tomorrow.' And as she said it, she knew she would.

'That's good,' he said warmly. 'Cause to celebrate.' He raised his glass. 'Cheers.'

'Cheers.' She smiled, the wine glowing inside her. 'I used to have a job, you know – a proper job. I was a rep with Happy Holidays – you know what that means?'

'Looking after the tourists, isn't it? Seeing they get to the right hotels, sort of thing.'

'Sort of.' She paused. 'It's where I met Colin – in Spain. Jesus!'

He raised his eyebrows.

'So corny,' she said bitterly. 'So bloody corny.'

He waited.

'So what about you, Ted?' she asked recklessly. The wine, thrown down too quickly, was making her light-headed. 'You've been married, haven't you?'

'Yes. Twice. Both disasters.'

'Oh, Ted – *Ted.* You shouldn't have done it.'

'I know. But it could be worse.'

'Could it?'

He nodded. 'I'm working with my daughter now. She's in charge of this shindig.'

'What shindig's that?' she asked, puzzled.

'The series. *Rowley's Patch.*'

'Oh, you mean the soap.'

'Yes, if you prefer.'

'That's unusual, isn't it – working with your daughter?'

'It is a bit. But it's not unprecedented.'

'Well, that's fine then. Just fine,' she cried, with an expressive gesture.

He frowned. 'Are you all right, Kate?'

'Of course I'm all right. But this wine's a bit – strong.' She put the glass down, with a sudden lurch. 'Sorry. But I think I'd better be going.'

'Sure. But would you like some coffee first?'

'No, I'll be fine – fine.' She got to her feet clumsily. 'What's her name, by the way – your daughter?'

'Carol.'

'Carol,' she repeated. 'That's a nice name. A sweet name. Give her my love.' She smiled flutteringly. 'Silly of me – she doesn't know me, does she?' She snorted. 'Goodbye, Ted – thanks for showing me round.'

'You haven't seen much.' He squeezed her hand, smiled. 'You'll come again, won't you?'

'Maybe I will. Maybe not.'

'Are you sure you're all right?' he asked anxiously. 'Shall I call you a cab? I'm afraid I don't drive, or I'd take you home.'

'You don't drive?' She swayed slightly. 'And you a TV writer? I don't believe it.'

'I'm afraid it's true. Look, sit down a minute.'

'No, I'm going. I'm all right. Really.' She seemed to gather herself together, walking firmly to the door. 'I'll see myself out – don't worry. Thanks for showing me around.'

He insisted, all the same, on accompanying her to the gate.

'You know, Ted,' she said thoughtfully. 'You're one of my heroes. Always have been.' Standing on tip-toe, she kissed him quickly on the cheek.

Back indoors, Trinder whimpered. 'Don't worry, boy,' he said, with a queer, twisted grin. 'It'll be OK.' He sat down heavily, feeling his age.

12

'You're looking pretty pleased with yourself,' said Carol bleakly.

'Am I?'

'Yes, you are. I won't ask why. Got that script?'

'Yes. Don't look so surprised,' replied Ted, wondering anew at the unpredictability of women. What was biting his daughter now?

In the outer office, the door between the rooms wide open as usual, Carol's PA, Elen Watkins, tip-tapped her computer. Ted briefly considered chatting her up, to prove he was still alive, but thought better of it, restrained by the knowledge of Carol's heavy disapproval of his doing any such thing. He sighed inwardly at the fierceness of contemporary women, especially successful women, his daughter included. They were a breed apart. He even spent a moment thinking nostalgically of his first wife, Jane Hart, Carol's mother, and a longer moment thinking of his second wife, Letty. The first divorced and dead, the second merely divorced. He stopped thinking, frozen by the look Carol was giving him.

'You don't have to, you know,' she said.

'What?'

'Sit there looking like a naughty schoolboy. You can go if you like.'

'Is that a dismissal?' He intended irony but realised his voice sounded only pathetic.

'It's a suggestion,' she said crisply, and turned back to the script she was scanning.

'Oh. Right.' He remained where he was for a few seconds until, feeling juvenile and unnecessary, he stood up with a half-hearted display of insouciance. 'I'll be on my way then. Let me know what you think.'

'I will, don't worry.'

He determined to leave without even a glance at Elen.

'The first two were fine,' conceded Carol, glancing up briefly as he went through the open door to the outer office. 'This looks OK too.'

'Oh. Thanks,' he said ironically, making a conspiratorial face at Elen. Bunched up at her console, she ignored him. 'Blow you then,' he said silently.

He made his way along a corridor bedevilled by grimacing portraits of Media City celebs to the canteen, which he refused to call by its grandiose title of 'staff restaurant', self-served himself a coffee and paid at a till occupied by a large, cheerful woman whose raucous Cardiff accent made him feel that all was not lost with the world. It was mid-morning in Media City, and the canteen was filling up. He found an empty table by the picture windows commanding broad views of the Welsh capital, with the Glamorgan hills in the distance. Words came to him, spoken by one of his characters: he had already begun writing the next script in his head. Then he became aware of being stared at and glanced up to see Conrad Matthews, Cambrian Television Press Officer, smiling across the tables at him. Ted looked away distastefully, but it was too late: the trap had been sprung. Conrad pushed his chair back and with the large, purposeful strides of an apprentice kangaroo lunged to Ted's table.

'Ted Sloane, by all that's wonderful! Just the man I've been looking for.' He looked lugubriously down at his prey, his eyes glittering like huge blue marbles behind his glasses. 'How's the big show coming on, OK?'

'It's not a show, it's a drama,' Ted replied coldly.

'Of course, of course. But you're the word man, not me.' Conrad's absurdly boyish face exuded goodwill as he pressed his pudgy white hands down hard on the back of the empty chair opposite. 'Look, old boy, I'm sorry to break in on you, but could you spare a mo' with Simon? You know him, don't you?'

'Yes, I'm afraid I do,' said Ted, with a sharp glance at the squat, bearded hack sharing Conrad's table. 'He's the shit who wrote that snide piece about me in the local rag, isn't he?'

'Well now, shit's a strong word –'

'It's the right one.'

'Yes, but *chwarae teg* now. Only doing his job, wasn't he? He's a gossip columnist, after all. Nothing personal in it, I'm sure.'

'Nor with me. I just don't want anything to do with him, that's all.'

'Well, that's unfortunate, Ted. Really unfortunate.'

'Why?'

'Well, you see, he's just taken over the telly page from Sarah Digby – you know Sarah, don't you? No? Never mind. The fact is, Ted, and I'm sure you'll understand – we can do with all the publicity we can get for *Rowley's*. Get people interested, you know? Lead up to a big support campaign. Fact is, Simon's keen on giving you a big write-up in the *Voice*. Celeb author signs up for Cambrian, sort of thing. It's a heaven-sent opportunity, Ted – just what Carol's looking for,' he said plaintively, as Ted's steely gaze began to erode his confidence. 'You don't have to do it now, of course – just come and say hullo, that's all. He's a big fan of yours, Simon – I can tell you that straight. All I want –'

'Bugger off, Conrad,' said Ted wearily.

'Now, Ted -'

'And bugger him too.'

Conrad's face underwent an extraordinary transformation as he snapped from one persona to another. 'That's not very clever, Ted – if I may say so.'

'Oh?'

'Not very clever at all.'

Suddenly he was sitting opposite, his speed of movement so swift that Ted scarcely noticed it.

'There's the little matter of – how shall I put it,' murmured Conrad, studying the fingernails of his right hand intently. 'The filial relationship? Mm?'

'Meaning?'

'It's all perfectly right and proper, of course. Quite above board. But a certain . . . *spin* can be put on these things, yes?'

'I wouldn't know. And I don't particularly care.'

'No, I can see. But just think about it, old boy. Have a word with Carol.'

He smiled, twisted away and was back with the man from the *Cardiff Voice* in a trice.

Ted Sloane, fuming, sat rigidly alone.

'Come in, old boy. Take a pew.' Sir Charles, beaming, gestured Colin to sit down. He put aside the *Telegraph* he'd been reading, with a flurry of its crisp broadsheet pages. 'You know, this paper isn't what it was. I was reading a piece in it the other day about lesbian marriages. Extraordinary. Anyway, how's Eaglefield? Everything sorted now, is it? Good. Now then, fancy a snifter? End of a hard day, isn't it? Time to relax. Scotch suit you?'

As he took the bottle from the drinks cabinet, Colin had a sudden image of himself in twenty years' time, too pink in the face, too round in the belly, too tired to do anything but dawdle through a working day shuffling papers, reading the *Telegraph* and pretending he was still important. It was not a pleasant prospect.

'Say when.'

'When.'

'Only a thimbleful,' Sir Charles chided. 'You'll hardly wet your lips with that, man. Well – bottoms up.'

'Cheers.'

Sir Charles sat back heavily. Colin's gaze was held now by a lock of white hair that intruded over his employer's brow; he felt it strange that he had not noticed before just how thick and curly his hair was, and by a sudden shifting of his sights he saw, not himself as an old man, but Sir Charles as a young one. What a wicked devil he must have been! Legends of his adulterous exploits of old still lingered in the business, as did tales – told with admiration and envy – of the way his young, thrusting firm had knocked out tired old rivals in the Sixties and given Cardiff a much-needed taste of modernism. But why hadn't he packed it all in by now? It was sad to see him still here, doing damn-all, leaving everything to others, simply unable to quit.

'Conference is coming up soon,' Sir Charles remarked buoyantly. 'Fancy going again this year?'

'If you like,' Colin carefully replied. 'Unless you want someone else to go, of course.'

'Oh? Who do you suggest?'

'Well . . .' Colin hesitated. 'Sharon?' His boss grimaced. 'Or Matthew, maybe?'

'Matthew's all right,' Sir Charles agreed, pointedly avoiding any comment on Sharon. 'But I'd prefer you to go. If you don't mind, that is.'

'No,' said Colin quickly. 'I don't mind in the least. When is it?'

Sir Charles gave him the dates then sat back, swivelling his chair sideways, his profile pensive, the tips of his fingers touching in a pious, semi-prayerful gesture.

'I wonder if you'd mind taking someone with you? Someone I think might benefit from the experience.' Colin looked at him questioningly. 'Yvonne,' said Sir Charles, swivelling his chair back as if to give the name emphasis.

Colin's heart thumped in a way that told him far more about himself than he had ever realised. 'Yvonne,' he repeated, as neutrally as he could.

'Don't look so surprised. She plays a big part in this operation, you know.'

'Oh, I know that but . . . Is it possible? I mean, she's not qualified, is she?'

'I can send who I like,' Sir Charles said severely. 'We'll put her down as your PA. Which she is, anyway. She's PA to us all.'

'Of course,' said Colin hastily. 'I'm not disputing that. Well, if you want her to go that's fine by me. No question of it.'

'Good. I think it'll be good for her in many ways – give her an insight into things. She'll make good contacts, too – they always come in useful.' He smiled blandly. 'Well,' he observed comprehensively, 'that's all settled then. I'll tell her to go ahead and make the arrangements. You'll be staying in the same hotel, of course – no objection, I assume? We'll book two en-suite rooms.' Adjoining, he added privately.

Alone again, Sir Charles let out a slow, ripe chuckle. 'Colin and Yvonne,' he murmured. 'You wicked old bugger, Lewis.' Absently, he picked up a muddy green paperweight shaped like a frog with addled eyes and tapped his desk with it, repetitively. He began humming to himself softly.

'The Gos is all right,' said Pam, whisking crumbs from her skirt onto the worn red carpet in the back room of the charity shop, 'if you don't take too much notice of her. If you do, she's a pain.'

'She seems OK,' protested Kate mildly, not wishing to upset her new colleague over lunchtime sandwiches, with the shop closed for an hour. 'She gave me a nice welcome at any rate.'

'That's because she's desperate to get you here, honey. Nothing personal, I assure you.'

Kate rode the put-down as best she could, suspecting that Pam did not intend it to be as insulting as it sounded.

'The trouble with Jill, dalling' – Kate had soon realised that for Pam, the 'r' in the word 'darling' was redundant – 'is that she's sex-starved. Her old man's got no more balls than a Hindu cow.'

'Really?' Kate smiled; the slender but shapely Pam clearly packed one hell of a verbal punch.

'You wait till you see him. He's the next best thing to a bag of wind I've ever seen in my life.'

Delicately she nibbled a bright red apple, her grey eyes solemn behind expensively-framed glasses. Pam, Kate had quickly discovered, wasn't short of a bob or two.

'But dalling,' effused Pam, 'don't let me put you off being here. It's good to have you – I was bored out of my pants with the Gos all day, with no-one to talk to. We'll have some fun, dalling.'

She smiled, and Kate felt sudden warmth for this intense and unpredictable woman. Perhaps coming to work here would be far better than she imagined.

At five to two Jill Gosport bustled back, giving Kate and Pam a keen glance, as if they might have been up to no good in her absence. ('You know what?' Pam confided. 'She gives that useless husband of hers a cooked lunch every day. Microwave job. Should put his bum in it one day. It's fat enough to feed an army.') The afternoon was far busier than Kate had expected, and for the first time in years she felt she was actually doing something worthwhile. She was tidying up a rack of clothes when she sensed rather than saw somebody scanning a shelf of paperbacks behind her. 'Alan Sillitoe,' a voice murmured. 'Can't I ever get rid of the bastard?'

She turned. 'What on earth are you doing here?'

'The same as anyone else,' Ted Sloane replied suavely. 'Don't need a passport to get in, do I?'

'No, but – it's my first day here. I didn't know you were coming.'

'I'll send you a card next time. Enjoying yourself?'

'Yes thanks.' Jill, busy serving, did not notice the new arrival, but Kate was conscious of Pam's keen scrutiny. 'I thought you'd be busy writing, this time of day,' Kate volunteered, feeling absurdly shy.

'No – I write in the morning. Afternoons I'm knackered.'

'So you've done your quota for today then, have you?'

'Oh, there's no quota. I just stop when I feel like it.'

Why was he so difficult? Kate fidgeted with the skirts and tops, lost for words.

'Look,' said Ted quickly. 'I was hoping you'd be here. I've brought you this – I forgot to give it you yesterday.' He handed her a paper bag. 'The signed copy you said you'd like, remember?'

'Oh – *thanks*. That *is* good of you.'

'Not at all. I'm very flattered.'

She took the book from the bag – *Eden's Rock,* his third novel.

'Don't read it all at once now,' he warned. 'It's got a government health warning.'

'Oh, Ted,' she began gratefully. 'I love this. The copy I've got's worn to shreds.'

'Then look after this one – there won't be another.' He smiled. ''Bye, Kate.'

She wanted to say 'Oh, don't go' but simply watched him walk out of the shop. She rearranged the clothes on the rack, pointlessly, feeling empty and angry with herself for not making more of the moment.

'Well, well,' murmured Pam, sidling up to her. 'Proper little dark horse, aren't we? Who's the dishy fellow then?'

'Oh – just someone I know,' Kate returned.

'You don't say! Doesn't he have a name then?'

'He's Ted,' said Kate reluctantly. 'Ted Sloane. He's an author.'

'An author! You mean he writes books?'

'Authors generally do,' replied Kate, getting one back with satisfaction. 'He was a big name once.'

'Not twice?' Pam's eyes gleamed with the swiftness of her riposte. 'What happened to him then, dalling?'

'I don't know . . . He went out of favour, I suppose.'

'Like chocolate buttons,' said Pam obscurely. 'But what's he doing here, dalling? He doesn't *live* here, does he?'

Kate was about to reply that authors have to live somewhere when Jill cut short their tête-à-tête. All girls together they might be, but she was the boss and, Kate soon discovered, she had her ways of making people know it.

Ffion Tomos would not do anything out of love for Gwynne Tecwyn, but she would do a lot out of regard for herself. As head of a PR consultancy she prided herself on being a fixer, and the prospect of lining up a confrontation between Jasper Taylor, hard man of TV, and the soft-centred First Minister of the Welsh Assembly was too delicious to resist. Of course, she couldn't do it herself; she would have to make use of her Contacts.

The word capitalised itself in her brain as did Martyrdom for Irish patriots and Bondage for sado-masochists. She loved contacts; she had an address book full of them. Contacts in county councils, town councils, arts bodies, colleges, schools, libraries, museums, sporting clubs, business clubs, big firms, small firms, any-size firms who might conceivably come up with some cash or collateral. All might come in useful some time; Ffion cast her net wide. At any time of day, and sometimes at night, someone of influence (however slight) might pick up the phone to hear Ffion's soft, slightly breathy voice discreetly suggest something that might be of mutual benefit. If it were a male that she telephoned, he might well deceive himself into thinking that for Ffion, he had a special magic and (were he extremely gullible) even held for her an erotic attraction. If it were a female, she would consider herself far more intelligent after the conversation than before. Ffion had the knack of making everyone feel her confidante; it was the secret of her success. But the contacts she loved best were those in the media, for, in her mind, the media equalled power

She drummed her long, exquisite fingers on her desk after drinking her second cup of black coffee of the morning before dialling a number and settling back comfortably.

'Clayton,' she said sweetly, 'how are you today, *cariad?* . . . Oh, I'm sorry to hear that, who's been stirring it this time? . . . Oh hell, you don't have to take that from anyone . . . Never mind, darling, look – could you spare me a minute? . . . No, it's not about the exhibition, I know you've done a piece about that. It's something else I've got in mind, something quite spicy . . . No, darling, not that kind of spice, it's politics we're talking about – broadly speaking . . . Yes, I know it's not but I do get about a bit and keep my ears open . . . you bet . . . Oh no, *cariad,* I can't possibly tell you over the phone, shall we meet somewhere? . . . No, not the club, that's just a wee bit too public . . . How about the Butchers, that suit you? Yes? One o'clock? . . . Yes, quarter-past will be fine . . . quarter to half-past, any time that suits you . . . 'Bye, *cariad,* goodbye . . .'

She closed her eyes beatifically, a fitting subject for Michelangelo.

13

'So you'll come then, will you?' said Joyce.

'I don't know. I might.'

Joyce glanced at Kate impatiently. 'What've you got to lose? It's only a party, for heaven's sake.'

She cupped her free hand firmly around the coffee mug, obliterating the cartoonist Gren's sheep frolicking through Aberflyarff with such slogans as 'Ban mint sauce' emblazoned on their woolly-jumper bodies.

'I'm not sure about Brendan, to be honest,' said Kate. 'He seems a bit . . . seedy.'

Joyce flicked back a stray lock of fair hair impatiently. 'Of course he's seedy. That's the whole point of him. It's because he's seedy that we're going.'

'I'll see what Colin thinks,' Kate replied, disguising the distaste she often felt for the sheer awfulness of Joyce, the blowsy vulgarity of her.

'Christ, Kate!' exclaimed Joyce, seeing through her. 'Anyone would think you were the Virgin Mary.'

Kate flushed.

'Oh, come on, Kate. It'll be a laugh. It's sure to be OTT, with pumpkins everywhere and witches' masks and God knows what. Oh, and there's something else – everyone's asked to bring a surprise guest along.'

'What's the point of that?'

'I don't know – just something different, I suppose. I don't know who I'll bring – the bloody bank manager, probably. He's just sent me a stinking letter – he can do with sweetening up.'

'Derek's not in the red, is he?' asked Kate, her equilibrium restored.

'No, he's not – I am.'

Kate, forever mystified by other people's domestic arrangements, let this pass.

'I know,' said Joyce, eyes suddenly mischievous. 'You can bring that famous author – the one you fancy.'

'I don't fancy him,' returned Kate hotly. 'I hardly know him.'

'You've seen him though, haven't you? You told me.'

'Yes but that's not *fancying*.'

Joyce's sharp, metallic laugh was like a dagger through Kate's skull. 'Methinks the lady doth protest too much,' she declared, revealing an acquaintance with Shakespeare which Kate would not have suspected. 'Come on, admit it – you've got the hots for him good and proper.'

Back in her own house, Kate's first instinct was to ignore the whole episode. But as she waited for Colin to come home (and he was getting later and later these days), she felt a resentment that made the diversion of a Hallowe'en party more and more appealing.

'So. The Discovery then, is it?' asked Colin casually.

'If you like. Wherever,' replied Yvonne.

He put his car into reverse, backed out of his parking place outside the office of the Charles Lewis Partnership in Cardiff Bay, and drove off into the damp October night. Yvonne, beside him, felt stiff and unnatural. She had never thought it would ever come to this, her romantic imaginings of a closer relationship with Colin actually made flesh. The first time they had gone to a pub together had been a spur-of-the-moment affair; this was more deliberate, a carefully arranged assignation for which she felt ill prepared.

Pent up in silence, hands clasped in her lap, she rested her head on the support above the front passenger seat where, she was now acutely aware, his wife's head must rest when they went out together. She shifted her head from side to side, as if to assert her right to be there. It was Colin who had asked her out, she reminded herself, without any scheming on her part. She hadn't manoeuvred in the least; it was entirely his doing.

Was this the beginning of an affair? she wondered. His manner suggested it. It was not so much anything he had said or did as small, indefinable things, the way he had held the car door open for her, the emanations of excitement she felt coming from him.

Sir Charles's suggestion that she should go to the London conference with Colin had come as a shock. 'Are you sure?' she had asked, scarcely believing her ears.

'Of course,' her boss had returned, frowning, as if the question implied some questioning of his authority. 'You want to progress your career, don't you?'

'Naturally,' said Yvonne, feeling a little foolish. But in the next day or two Colin had been on edge, hardly looking at her. Then had come his idea of their going for a drink after work, implying (not at all successfully) that it entailed simply a discussion of business matters.

They stopped at traffic lights. 'Like some music?' he asked.

'Mm?' She glanced at him; he shoved a cassette in. The loud, emphatic music took her by surprise. He caught her startled look. 'Bartok. You know it?' She shook her head. The urgent rhythms had a strange, exalting effect. She no longer cared who she was or what she was doing; the passionate music possessed her entirely.

'You like it?'

'It's weird.'

'I take it that's a yes.'

She gave him a swift, uneasy glance. Was this such a good idea after all? 'What do you listen to – from choice?'

'What you'd call rubbish,' she said defensively. 'Oasis, Manic Street Preachers – stuff like that.' She hated the way she sounded. Why put herself down like this?

'Nothing wrong with that. I like the Manics myself.'

She felt he was humouring her, and stayed mute as they drove through the brightly-lit city centre to the tall Victorian houses of Roath. They swished past the stuccoed house where she had her third-floor flat and, glancing up, she wondered briefly what Chris (now decidedly her ex-boyfriend) was doing that moment in Swansea. Lulled by a quieter passage in the music, she felt a small, malicious pleasure in having so emphatically ditched him, just before this new phase of her life had caught her up in its infinite possibilities.

'You live round here, don't you?' asked Colin unexpectedly.

'Yes. We've just passed my place.'

'Oh. Why didn't you say?'

'I don't know. Seemed no point.'

The words, once out, seemed unduly harsh, as if she

were keeping him at a distance. 'It's only a flat,' she said. 'But it suits me OK.'

'Been there long?'

'Just over a year.'

'Mm-hm.'

They were groping for words to ease a tension between them that had never existed in the office.

'You live in Hollybush, don't you?'

'Yes – right on the edge. It suits us fine – you can go for walks in the country.'

How sweet, she thought with sudden, unexpected viciousness. *But what would the little woman think now if she saw me with her precious husband?* And then she reproved herself, *Steady on, girl.* The ghost of the wife she scarcely knew floated away, a wraith so insubstantial that it could not possibly harm her.

Past Roath Park Lake, where overfed ducks waddled unseen in the darkness, and with fingertip control he turned right at the roundabout and drove uphill past boxy houses of brutal Sixties architecture to a pub standing opposite a row of functional neighbourhood shops.

He glimmered a smile at her. 'You've been here before, of course?'

'No. Actually I haven't.'

'Haven't you?' He looked surprised. 'Well, time we put that right, isn't it?'

'Why The Discovery?' she asked, as they walked from the car to the pub. 'What are they discovering?'

'Themselves, usually. Like us.' He smiled again, enigmatically.

The Discovery was the nearest thing the Lakeside estate had to a heart. It was the place where the aspiring middle classes brought their partners, taking their mistresses or paramours further afield. It served well-kept ales and (in a different sense) well-kept people. Midweek, the pub was busy but they found a table to themselves. 'You know what this place is named after, of course,' Colin said, setting down his pint and Yvonne's spritzer. 'Captain Scott and all that.'

'Who was he?'

'Scott of the Antarctic. You mean you've never heard of him?' His amazement leapt up several notches.

'I'm afraid not. Is that terrible?'

'It's incredible. What did they teach you at school?'

'Oh, deportment – knitting,' she said dryly. 'Stupid things like that.'

'I'm sorry, Yvonne – I didn't mean to sound uppity. But I'm still surprised. I thought everyone knew – especially in Cardiff.'

'I'm a Jack, remember.'

'A what?'

'A Swansea Jack.'

'Oh.' Now it was his turn to look baffled. 'I'm sorry – I don't get it.'

'Swansea and Cardiff hate each other, don't they? Like chalk and cheese.' Or Hansel and Gretel, she added inwardly, absurdly.

'But all the same . . . you know the thing that looks like a lighthouse, don't you? In Roath Park Lake?'

'Yes, of course.' She frowned. 'It's a clock though, isn't it?'

'Well, it looks like a lighthouse. The point is, it commemorates Captain Scott and his men – they sailed to the South Pole from Cardiff. It says so on the plaque.'

'I've never bothered to read it,' Yvonne confessed. 'You must think me very stupid.'

'Not at all – of course I don't. I'm assuming too much, that's all. I suppose it's because I'm older than you.'

'Oh yes,' she said gravely. 'You're a real Methuselah.'

He smiled, relaxed. 'There's some photos of the expedition on the wall there,' he said, nodding in their direction. 'If you're interested.'

'What happened to them all then?'

'They died. Froze to death.'

'Ugh.'

'"I'm taking a little walk, and will be back in five minutes,"' Colin misquoted. She looked at him queryingly. 'That's what Oates said,' he explained. 'He just walked out into the blizzard.'

'I don't think I want to hear any more, thanks. It sounds horrible.'

'It is.' He supped his pint.

'Where are you now, Colin?' she asked suddenly. 'I mean – officially.'

He stiffened. 'Working late.'

'You don't feel guilty?'

'Why should I? That's what we're doing, isn't it?'

'Not really. If we're honest.' She gave him a direct look. ' Are we?'

He shrugged. 'There's the conference to discuss.'

'Come on, Colin,' she chided.

Something in her eyes reassured him. 'You don't object then?'

'Not in the least.'

'Good.'

The looks they exchanged cut through all the pretence and shilly-shallying that had characterised the beginnings of the new relationship they were establishing. Simultaneously, they noticed physical things about

117

each other that had so far escaped their attention: the small scar above his right eye, the way her left ear lobe was slightly askew.

'Have you told your wife? About the conference?' she asked.

'Of course.'

'And about me?'

He paused. 'No.'

'Then don't.'

'*Rowley's Patch*,' said Carol irritably. '*Rowley's* bloody *Patch*.' The three men seated in her office exchanged uneasy glances. 'It's a bloody awful title, isn't it? We'll have to think of another.'

'It's only a working title,' said Jarman, the project co-ordinator. 'We can always change it.'

'We'll have to. If we don't, we're in deep shit before we start.'

Baxter, the forward planner, put in nervously: 'How about *Valleys People*?'

Carol stared at him. '*Valleys People? Valleys People?* Christ.'

'I'm sorry,' said Baxter. 'It's only a suggestion.'

'If that's all you can suggest, Doug –'

'*Punters*,' interrupted Ted.

All eyes turned to him.

'That's your title,' he said.

'*Punters*,' repeated Jarman uncertainly, with the merest glance at Carol.

'H'm,' said Baxter. Silence caught at his throat.

'*Punters*,' said Carol coolly. She smiled. 'Ted, I think that might do rather nicely.'

The Butchers had been in Llandaff village as long as the camera had been in existence, and possibly long before that. Old photographs often depicted it, a wayside inn with thatched roof and horse trough, the unkempt road outside rutted by the wheels of farmers' carts and rich men's broughams. Its popularity had remained undimmed with the passage of time, and now it was the haunt not of farmers and burgesses but of restless media people, especially from the nearby BBC. They dropped in for quick lunchtime drinks and snacks, or longer after-work sessions before going home feeling more satisfied with the booze than they ever were with their jobs. If they felt inclined towards more spiritual comforts, the cathedral was near enough for them to totter downhill to this ancient edifice where Epstein's awesome sculpture, *Christ in Majesty*, seemed to float above the nave, as if upheld by angels. Llandaff, a tiny cathedral city on the fringe of large, blustering Cardiff, was cool, self-contained, a little aloof, more than a little precious.

Ffion Tomos sat alone in the back bar, drinking a Martini and ignoring everyone else as there was nobody present who could be the slightest use to her. No-one would have dreamed of disturbing the aura of unapproachability she exuded. She had the looks and the air of the subject of an old religious painting: a woman in this world but not quite of it, absorbing what she wished of her surroundings but essentially detached, on a different plane even.

Clayton Lloyd arrived five minutes late, nervy and harassed, edgy with explanations but not really listening either to himself or to Ffion until, as the yeasty brew began to work its magic, he became something (but not too much) like the mature, balanced broadcasting executive of his imagination.

'I like the idea,' he admitted eventually, 'but I'm not sure I can help you, Ffion *bach.*'

'Oh?' Ffion's hazel eyes expressed surprise, her well-modulated voice perfect confidence in her interlocuter.

'You see,' Clayton continued, restraining himself with difficulty from pressing his calves against hers beneath the table top, 'we have very little influence in London these days. Not that we've ever had much,' he added mournfully.

He ran his fingers through the wings of grey hair that brushed his large pink ears. Straggly sideburns confirmed the impression he gave of one clinging to a past in which he had been someone of promise.

'But as Head of News, Clayton –' began Ffion, halting as he shook his head.

'Not so, *cariad.* ACCA. As from yesterday.' Ffion raised her eyebrows. 'Assistant Controller, Current Affairs,' he explained.

'Oh, congratulations,' gushed Ffion, although perfectly aware that, at best, this was an ambiguous advancement. 'That means you've got even more power than before. All those contacts in Television Centre,' she hurried on, ignoring the slow shaking of Clayton's head, the irony in his thin-lipped smile. 'And you wouldn't mind seeing Rupert put on the spot, would you?' she added, very quietly.

'Rupert?' he repeated, his focus sharpening. 'What Rupert?'

'There's only one Rupert,' she returned, quite accidentally pressing his adventurously extended shoe with her own before, with exquisite modesty, folding her legs beneath her chair. 'Isn't there?'

'The First Minister,' Clayton breathed. 'Bastard.'

'Well then.' Ffion's moist, lustrous eyes held his.

Clayton, drawing on reserves of strength unsuspected by his detractors, drank deeply of his bitter. 'But Jasper Taylor,' he murmured uneasily. 'I don't know.'

Ffion traced the edge of her glass with a slender white finger. 'You did him a favour with that Welsh Development interview,' she observed. 'He owes you one, surely.'

'He may and he may not,' said Clayton. 'It depends on the way he sees it. He's a prickly customer.'

'Don't I know it,' she said feelingly, as if she had suffered conspicuously at the hands of a TV celebrity she had never spoken to in her life.

Clayton seemed impressed. 'Well then. You know how difficult it is.' He fiddled with his beer mat. 'I'll think about it,' he said eventually.

'Good!' exclaimed Ffion, with a look of infinite gratitude.

'Of course,' said Clayton sharply, as if already regretting his concession. 'It isn't a strong enough line in itself – the relationship you're talking about. That's not enough to make him bite.'

'Oh, I know that,' acknowledged Ffion sweetly. 'But I'm sure you can think of other ways for Jasper to squeeze his nuts. Can't you?'

'I can try.'

'That's my boy.'

14

It seemed to Kate that Colin was absolutely blind to the book she was reading. She left it lying around in conspicuous positions; held it up as she read it, so that he could hardly avoid seeing the cover; she cleared her throat as she turned a page, defying him *not* to notice. But he appeared wholly unaware that she was immersed in Ted Sloane's *Eden's Rock* yet again – not the old copy she had possessed for years but one so new-looking that it might have come straight from the printers. Oh, if only he would notice! Then she could reveal it to be a copy signed by the author, and admit that she had actually been in his house and drunk a glass of wine with him, and might well do so again because they had got on like a house on fire.

But did she really want him to know all that? How much *would* she tell him?

When she reflected on such matters, there was a strange emptiness where her stomach ought to be, and she was no nearer knowing the answer than explaining Einstein's Theory of Relativity. She would decide what to say when he asked, and let the spirit guide her.

But he did not ask. And it dawned on her that he knew very well what she was reading; that he had opened the book when she was out of the room, and seen Ted's signature on the title page; that he was deliberately not asking because he did not wish the fact of his knowing to enter their lives; but for what reason?

Their dual duplicity acted on them both, drawing them further apart and plunging them irrevocably into their secrets.

'Do you feel like going to the party on Saturday week?' Kate asked nonchalantly.

'What party's that?'

'The Hallowe'en Party. I told you about it.'

'I don't remember that. Where is it?

'At Brendan's.'

'Brendan's?' repeated Colin blankly.

'Don't look like that.'

'Brendan Collins?'

'Who else? You know him much better than me. He's in your golf club, isn't he?'

'What would we be going to his party for?'

'Because he's asked us. Jesus, Colin, what world are you living in?'

'I wouldn't go near one of his parties. He's a nasty old sod. Anyway I can't. I'm away then. I've got this conference in London.'

'What conference?'

'The Guild of Architects. I told you.'

'I don't remember that,' said Kate, unconsciously echoing his words.

'Well, I did.'

Kate, confused, was silent a moment or two before saying, 'Can't someone else go?'

'Why should they?' he returned, amused. 'Just so we can go to a Hallowe'en Party?'

'There's Sharon,' said Kate stubbornly. 'Why doesn't she go? She doesn't seem to do very much in that office.'

'She does as much as anyone. Why, what have you got against Sharon?'

'Nothing, she just seems such a hanger-on, that's all.'

'Hanger-on? What d'you mean?'

'Oh, I don't know. I'm just sick of the whole damn business, that's all.'

She blasted the TV with the remote so that the programme they weren't really watching was wiped away, leaving a silence filled with their separate, alien identities.

'Charles wants me to go, darling,' he said, in a reasonable tone of voice. 'I can't very well refuse.'

'Of course not,' she returned sarcastically. 'If he asked you to jump through a hoop you'd do it.'

'That's not fair, Kate.'

'Isn't it? It seems very fair to me.'

'He is the boss, after all.'

'Oh, is he? I thought he was the tea boy.'

'Now you're being stupid.'

'Of course I'm being stupid. I'm always bloody stupid. I don't know why you married me. It wasn't my brains, was it? All you wanted was an easy fuck.'

His face expressed, for an instant, his shock and distaste for her remark. She saw this spasm and raged, 'Is she going with you? She is, isn't she? I can see it on your face. God!'

How could she know about Yvonne, he wondered wildly.

'You're sleeping with her, aren't you? Admit it. Bloody hell, *Sharon.*'

In the joy of sheer relief Colin said, 'Don't be stupid, darling. Sharon isn't coming with me. Anyway, I wouldn't touch her with a barge-pole.'

'Oh, no. Very likely.'

'What gave you that idea? I don't even like the woman.'

'That doesn't stop you screwing her.'

'Well, I'm not. Do you hear me? I am *not* screwing Sharon.'

'Well, why are you so late home these days then?'

'How often am I late?'

'Quite often.'

'Wednesday I was, I know – we had a meeting with the Eaglefield lot. That'll be over soon, don't worry.'

'I've seen the way she looks at you. I hate her. And that voice of hers! I don't know how you stand it.'

'Sharon's harmless, darling. She's just got a few problems, that's all.'

'She's a man-eater. I know the type.'

'No, she's not,' Colin said indulgently, luxuriating in his reprieve.

'Oh, defending her now, are you?'

'No, but – be fair now. She's divorced, her daughter's gone off the rails and she's got a mother with Alzheimers. Life's not easy for her.'

'You seem to know a lot about her,' Kate said suspiciously.

'No more than anyone else in the office. That's common knowledge.'

Kate mulled this over. Secretly, she was glad that he couldn't get to the party because that would make it far easier for her to invite Ted as her surprise guest. But she wasn't going to let him off the hook that easily.

'So you swear you aren't going to London with Sharon?'

'I swear.'

Kate gunned the TV into life again. They watched it in silence.

'So you're really going to ask him to the party?' said Joyce, in the health food café she sometimes patronised during one of her sorties into Cardiff's late-Victorian shopping arcades.

'Yes. Why not?' replied Kate.

Joyce shrugged. 'I never thought you would, that's all.' She nibbled another slice of chopped-up lettuce, and pushed the plate away distastefully. She would never make a vegetarian: she had enjoyed the Sunday roast of her childhood too much, the lamb with mint sauce and baked potatoes that followed her father's sermon in the Aberystwyth chapel where the pews glowed with virtue; but the cellulose had to be fought, the dietary discipline maintained. She wiped her mouth with a serviette, which she crunched up and placed on top of her half-eaten green salad. 'Do you think he'll come?'

'I don't know. I'll have to ask him, won't I?'

'What makes you think he will? You hardly know him, do you?'

Kate hesitated, then took the plunge. 'I know him a lot better than you think.'

Joyce's antennae for scandal were instantly beamed at her friend. 'Oh yes?'

'He asked me in one day last week. Just for a drink and a chat.'

'You've been in his *house?*'

'Yes. Don't look like that. It was all innocent.'

'Come on, Kate. Nothing's innocent where men are concerned. You know that.'

'Well, this was,' said Kate stubbornly, although the faintest of blushes suggested otherwise.

'What did you talk about,' asked Joyce sarcastically, 'the birds and the bees?'

'If you're going to be like that, Joyce –'

'Come on, love. Can't you take a bit of teasing? Tell me, what happened? I'm all agog.'

'Nothing happened. We just talked about his books.'

Joyce's peal of laughter attracted glances from the next table. 'Then you went to see his etchings, did you? Kate, you're priceless.'

'I'm sorry I told you now,' said Kate, furious with herself.

'Oh, don't get in a huff. I'm sorry. Please.' Joyce leaned across the table, put a hand on her friend's arm. 'I'm just jealous, sweetheart, that's all. Nothing like that ever happens to me. Tell me all about it now. From the beginning. I'm all ears.'

'There's nothing much to tell,' protested Kate. But tell her she did, and Joyce listened – first with unconcealed delight, but increasingly with a troubled expression. 'Does Colin know about all this?' she asked.

'No.'

'None of it?'

'No.'

'Are you going to tell him?'

'Don't be stupid.'

'You're starting an affair.'

'No I'm not.'

'What is it then?'

Kate shrugged. 'I don't know. Have we got to put a name to everything?'

'I just have,' Joyce said pointedly. She was a little shocked, though not entirely surprised, to see the contemptuous look that swept unchecked across Kate's face, a look that told her something about their relationship that she had been hitherto unwilling to acknowledge.

'You think in clichés,' said Kate.

'Maybe I do. But it's a cliché situation, isn't it? Bored housewife has a fling with celebrity.'

Kate flushed. 'I can't believe you said that.'

Joyce shrugged.

Kate struggled for self-control. 'I suppose you and Derek will have a good laugh over this tonight, won't you?'

'We might – if I told him,' said Joyce calmly. 'But I shan't, don't worry.'

Kate gave her a look that said, *Tell me another.*

'You don't believe me, do you? Well, please yourself.'

Joyce sipped her coffee. Rarely did she enjoy such an advantage over Kate. She made the most of it, driving Kate deeper into the depths of self-reproach and resentment.

'Call for you, Ted,' called Elen Watkins from her desk. 'Will you take it?'

Dozing over the *Guardian* in Carol's inner sanctum, Ted shrugged himself awake. 'Who is it?' he called back.

'Someone called Kate Dawson.'

'Never heard of her.'

'I'll say you're at a meeting then.'

'Right . . . *no!*' he cried, cottoning on. 'Put her through . . . Hullo? . . . *Kate*, how are you? . . . Good. How's the job going? Like it there, do you? . . . You certainly looked at home . . . Don't worry, my pleasure . . . Well, I'm glad. Really . . .'

He listened, intrigued, to her proposition. Carol

128

bustled in, sat at her desk, glanced curiously at her father as he continued the conversation.

'Of course I'll come with you. I don't think I've ever been to a Hallowe'en party before. I'm very flattered . . . Not at all, the pleasure's mine . . . Look, why don't you come round here for coffee tomorrow morning? There's a very passable canteen . . . Why not? They don't bite, even if they *do* work in television . . . No, nonsense, not in the least . . . You know where we are, don't you? Just come to reception and ask for me . . . oh, eleven or thereabouts.' He caught Carol's expression. 'No, on second thoughts – make it half-past. I've got a meeting earlier. . . That's it then! Half-eleven tomorrow morning. And thanks for the invite. Smashing. 'Bye.'

Elen stood in the doorway, smiling.

'And who the hell's that?' asked Carol, with a steely expression.

Ted beamed. 'Our new character.'

The two women exchanged mystified glances.

15

Jasper Taylor was having a bad day. His train from Reading had been delayed by leaves on the line, or something equally ridiculous. Moreover, there'd been a letter from his ex's solicitors, demanding an upping of the already hugely inflated maintenance he paid her. And there'd been minor irritations, such as an absurd piece in *The Independent* taking a sideways swipe at him and, a balance in some ways but equally annoying, the more-than-usually-deferential manner of the commissionaires at his prestigious but often depressing workplace.

He sat, a small, hunched figure, in the *Taylor Tonight* office, four storeys up in the glassy new TV palace where he had been transmogrified from obscure academic into national icon. He was reading *The Guardian* now; he fed on the papers as a vampire feeds on human blood, and with an equal sense of inevitability. He heaved a deep, sad sigh, and cast it aside. It's not a holiday I need, he thought soberly; it's a day trip to Oblivion.

It was the witching hour when the programme was shaping up and the afternoon conference looming. He had no objection to the main item or what would probably be the second, a running story they couldn't very well ignore. It was the lightweight piece about the Welsh Assembly he had bridled at. Not *again?* he had protested. We did them not long ago, didn't we? . . .

Well, three months, four months, what did it bloody matter, there was no *story* there worth talking about. And Rupert Fallon, for godsake, not Rupert *Fallon* again. The man was a bad actor, with his pseudo-RADA accent and floppy bow ties. What had the Welsh nats come to, electing a man like this as their leader? And he was First Minister now, for Chrissake, after the total humiliation of Labour in the election. What could they talk about? Who'd be interested? Anyway he couldn't stand the Welsh, had never had any time for them. Well, that *could* be an advantage, he privately admitted, after the duty editor had greased him up a bit. Wouldn't mind putting the little squirt on the rack. But were they *sure* this wasn't common knowledge in Wales? Anyway, what did it matter? . . . Oh well, as a payoff, a bit of piss-taking of the Taffia . . . might be a bit of fun he supposed . . . OK, he'd do it. Put the Welsh lamb up for slaughter.

In fact, he decided, perking up as he always did as they reached the point of no return, he'd get a real kick out of taking the wind out of Rupert's dodgy sails. Whistling softly, he went for a pizza.

Ffion was getting more than a little bored with Gwynne Tecwyn. He took a lot for granted, not least his supposed mastery in the bedroom. Privately she thought of him as two-minute Tecwyn, but outwardly she indulged him, massaging his ego with the duplicity that served her so well in her professional life. Ffion had learned to keep her emotional distance the hard way. At nineteen she had fallen destructively for a married man, a disaster that had shocked her father far more than her highly practical mother. Daniel and

131

Gwenyth Thomas had privately grieved over the aborted foetus, the lost grandson or granddaughter who would by now be in high school. Gwenyth prayed for the child's soul, believing that even an unborn foetus had a right to immortality.

'I can't wait for this,' Gwynne said gleefully, sprawled on her modish two-seater settee. 'Are you sure he's going to do it?'

'No, I'm not. How can I be? But Clayton says he will.'

'Clayton Lloyd,' mocked Gwynne. 'Bloody hell. Right old fart he is.' He raised and lowered one arm, pinching his nose with the other.

Ffion's distaste for him plumbed new depths. She wondered why she had gone to such lengths to please this oaf, yet knew the answer already: she had done it for her own satisfaction, not his, to prove herself so completely a mistress of manipulation. Ffion took pride in her reputation as a woman who made things happen; who else could have cooked up so effortlessly the succulent treat that awaited them? Rupert Fallon, leader of Plaid Cymru, was about to be kebabbed by Jasper Taylor, scourge of the chattering classes!

'Great little Chablis this,' said Gwynne pointedly, twirling the nearly-empty glass. 'Where d'you get it, Oddbins?'

'No, Tesco's. And if you want another you can pour it yourself.'

He glared at her. 'What's biting you? Thought you'd be over the moon, with all this.'

'Over the moon!' she repeated scornfully. 'I'm not a football manager, Gwynne.'

'Very funny.' Heaving himself forward, he grabbed the bottle by its throat and sloshed wine generously into his glass. A few more mouthfuls restored his composure. 'Only an hour to go,' he said smugly. 'Come and sit by me, *cariad.*' He patted the empty place at his side.

'In a minute,' said Ffion. She tweaked open the curtain of her first-floor maisonette to look over the still, silent waters of Cardiff Bay. An unusual feeling possessed her, an unease, too slight to be called remorse, at what she had done. This stemmed not from sympathy with Rupert Fallon, whom she regarded as an odious little poseur, but from a growing sense of the reality of the writer of whom she had never heard until recently. Unexpectedly, he had become a shadowy figure at the edge of her consciousness, a man who (she had learned) had once been famous but was now no more than a hack TV scriptwriter. How could anyone fall so low and still retain any self-respect? The question intrigued her and, in the past few days, she had found herself wanting to put flesh on the shadowy figure who was still little more for her than a mere idea. What might become of him after Jasper Taylor had taken Rupert apart, she wondered. Would Ted Sloane really suffer from this exposure of the nepotism so rife in the New Wales?

Glancing at Gwynne Tecwyn squatting frog-like in front of the telly, waiting for Taylor the Terrible to do his worst, she wondered why she had bothered to intervene in the lives of this unknown man and his daughter. And all for this buffoon!

She let the curtain fall back into place, refilled her glass and sat beside him, silently.

In spite of all the efforts of TV make-up departments, Rupert Fallon always contrived to look exceedingly pink when well pleased with himself. And five minutes into the interview on *Taylor Tonight,* he felt very pleased with himself indeed. He had warded off numerous thrusts of the notorious Taylor rapier; countered snide remarks with cool self-possession; turned his persecutor's effrontery to his own advantage, showing him up to be (so he imagined) the arrogant bore that he was. His round face turned plum-coloured with self-satisfaction; his spotless bow tie was the acme of sophistication; he was totally in control. He especially congratulated himself on the way he had dealt with that hoary old topic of cottage burnings in the Welsh-speaking heartlands. He was coasting, boy, coasting.

And then came the softly-posed question that set alarm bells ringing in his head as soon as they were uttered. 'So the Taffia no longer exists in Wales – is that what you're saying?' asked Jasper sardonically.

'I don't know what you mean by the Taffia,' Rupert unhesitatingly replied.

'Oh, come along, Mr Fallon, you know very well what I mean – the doing of favours, the back-scratching, the golden inner circle who've been running Wales since the year dot.'

'I don't accept your premise in the least. And if I may say, it's insulting of you to suggest it.'

'Is it now? I wonder. Because I'm sure you're aware that there are odd juxtapositions so far as certain jobs are concerned.'

'Are there? I'm not aware of it.'

'Are you not? Then are you familiar with the name Ted Sloane, Mr Fallon?'

'Ted Sloane?' Rupert's brow furrowed. 'No, I don't think I am.'

'That's extraordinary. At one time he was a luminary of the Angry Young Man school of writing – you've heard of that, I assume.'

'Vaguely,' replied Rupert, after a pause.

'Only vaguely? You surprise me. But I suppose the fact that they didn't write in Welsh puts them outside the orbit of your experience.'

'Not necessarily,' retorted Rupert, turning a deeper shade of pink.

'Well, the fact is, Mr Fallon, that Ted Sloane is now employed as script editor – sorry,' Jasper sneeringly corrected, 'script *consultant* – for a new soap opera emanating from Cambrian Television – you've heard of *that* company, I suppose?'

'Of course. But I fail to see the relevance of all this.'

'Do you now. The relevance, Mr Fallon, is in the fact that the man's immediate boss happens to be his very own daughter – doesn't that strike you as odd?'

'It may or may not be – it depends on the circumstances.'

'Naturally.'

'You're not suggesting there is anything improper in this appointment, are you?' asked Rupert sharply.

'Not in the least. Just unusual. And I can give you other examples, going back down the years. Isn't it true that at one time no teacher could expect a headship in Glamorgan unless he belonged to a particular party?'

'That was the Labour Party,' countered Rupert instantly.

'Not yourselves?'

'No.'

'So that made it all right, did it?'

'Not at all. I'm merely stating . . .' floundered Rupert.

'The Taffia rules, doesn't it, Mr Fallon?'

'Not in the least.'

'Very well, let's move on to other matters . . .'

Gwynne Tecwyn clapped his hands exultantly. 'That's nailed her! By God, that's done for her good and proper!' He gave a wild whoop, and turned to impart a congratulatory kiss upon Ffion's lips. Sinuously she veered away and made precipitately for the bathroom, where she looked hatefully at her reflection. 'Stupid bitch,' she breathed. 'Common bitch.' The word 'common' was a self-laceration far more severe than the 'stupid.'

16

Driving to the TV studios, Kate felt a mixture of excitement and fear. She could not believe she had summoned up the courage to phone Ted the previous day. If Colin hadn't got up her nose so much over that trip of his to London – if she hadn't been so damned suspicious of him these days – she'd never have done it. Sharon – God! Her voice was enough to make a plastic madonna break wind. But he fancied her, in her bones she knew he fancied her. And she'd fancied *him* for years, that was obvious. That Christmas party she'd gone to, with that obscene old deadbeat Charlie Lewis lording it over them all . . . he'd caught the looks she'd been giving him, the old come-and-get-me. Colin hadn't obviously responded, he'd been the faithful-to-death spouse then – she couldn't believe now that she'd hated that side of him – but now . . . She had visions of them in London together, booking into a hotel – would they have separate rooms or go for a double right off? – of course she could ask where he'd be staying, then call the hotel when he was there, but what would that prove? She couldn't ask if he'd booked a double, could she? And even if she could, she wouldn't. She was too proud. If he wanted to do it, let him do it. See if she cared. And two could play at that game, couldn't they? The thought, crossing her mind, made her hands go clammy on the wheel and her stomach lurch. Would she?

She felt so distracted that she almost got into the wrong lane at the busy intersection near Media City, HQ of Cambrian Television. The car behind her blared and she stuck up two fingers at the driver, hoping he'd see it through the back window. He blared again, longer this time and, stuck at the lights just before the roundabout, she was afraid for a moment that he'd get out and shout at her through her side window. Just to be on the safe side, she pushed down the inside lock. The lights changed and she shot forward so quickly that she had to brake hard to avoid going into the van in front. *Calm down, Kate, for heaven's sake . . .* Suddenly she was overcome by the feeling she was trying so hard to set aside, the desire to shut herself away and have as little to do with people as she could. She gripped the steering wheel tightly. She would *not* turn round and drive away, she would *not*. At last the feeling subsided. Briskly she swung the car through the open, wrought-iron gates and began looking for a parking space.

Ted Sloane had got along thus far without a car, and he had no intention of changing that state of affairs. The idea of propelling a chunk of potentially lethal metal through crowded streets had always filled him with horror. It was to avoid traffic that he had chosen to live a little out of town when he moved to Cardiff, and this was no inconvenience as the nearest bus stop was only a few minutes' walk away. If he took a taxi to the studio, he could be there in twenty minutes. But generally, there was no need to rush; he was a scriptwriter, not a company man under pressure.

The morning after the TV kebabbing of the First Minister, a programme he had missed because he would no more willingly watch Jasper Taylor than grapple with the gears of a Ferrari, he arrived at Media City to find Julie at reception giving him a keener look than usual.

'Morning Julie,' he said heartily, waving his pass in his usual airy manner. 'Everything OK?'

'Yes thanks. And you?'

'Excellent.'

'Good,' she said, but as he smiled back he detected something a little strange – could it be disappointment? – in her manner. He thought nothing of it until, reaching Carol's office, he found Elen Watkins there alone, giving him exactly the kind of look he had received at reception.

'Where's Carol?' he asked cheerfully.

Elen jabbed a finger at the ceiling.

'Oh? Who with?'

'Arnold, of course.'

'Why of course?'

'You don't know? You mean you didn't see the programme?'

'What programme?'

Wordlessly she passed him that morning's *Western Mail.* He read, swiftly and disbelievingly:

Jasper Taylor attacked the so-called 'Taffia' in a hard-hitting interview with Welsh First Minister Rupert Fallon in his Taylor Tonight TV programme last night.

He alleged favouritism at Cambrian TV – because head of drama Carol Hart gave her father, Ted Sloane, a top job as script consultant.

Hart leads the team producing the forthcoming soap Punters – with former best-selling novelist Sloane in charge of scripting.

Hart and Sloane were unavailable for comment last night, but a spokesperson for Cambrian TV said . . .

'This is bloody stupid!' Ted exploded. 'I'll sue the bastards for libel.'

'I think you should,' said Elen gleefully. 'Not very nice, is it?'

'Nice! I should say it's not nice. What did Carol say?'

'She hit the roof. Arnold's none too pleased either, from what I gather.'

'I'll go up and see him now. They can't get away with this.'

'I shouldn't if I were you. Leave it to Carol.'

'Why?'

'Because she wants you to. She tried to get you on the phone, but you'd left.'

'I didn't know a thing about it. Did you see it?'

'No, I was out. Good job you and Carol are ex-directory. They were after you last night.'

'Who?'

'The press of course. Seen Conrad's statement?'

'Yes. *Perfectly acceptable professional arrangement,*' said Ted derisively.

'Well, he did his best, didn't he?'

'Some best!'

They sat in uncomfortable silence until Carol returned from her meeting with the MD, looking cool and unflappable. 'Hullo,' she said brightly. 'Enjoy the show?'

'Fuck the show. What are we doing about it?'

'Nothing.'

'Nothing! You've seen this?' His finger stabbed the paper. 'It's bloody libellous.'

'Don't be silly. It's just flim-flam.'

'What? All this talk of the Taffia?'

'Calm down, Ted. It's only Jasper sounding off. You

140

know what a dick-head he is. It'll all be forgotten tomorrow.'

'Oh, will it now.'

'Yes. If we don't make a fuss. If we do it'll go on and on. Least said, soonest mended.'

'Oh, thank you very much,' said Ted sarcastically. 'So much for your reputation.'

'Your reputation's safe. So is mine. Arnold's backing us, that's the main thing. But we need something from you.'

'From *me*?'

'Yes. A bit of collateral.'

'What are you talking about?'

'An interview in the press. All this could be good publicity.'

'Like hell it can! Count me out.'

'That's not very clever, Ted. Think about it.'

Ted gave his daughter a long look. 'Conrad Matthews has been getting at you, hasn't he? I saw him in the canteen last week.'

'He's had a word or two with me, yes.'

'I don't know how you can stand the swine. He gives me the creeps.'

'He's all right when you get to know him.'

'Do me a favour, Carol. He's six foot of sheer crap. Where'd they find him, anyway? He's never been on a paper in his life, I bet.'

'I wouldn't know. Press office is nothing to do with me, is it?'

'He was a teacher,' interposed Elen Watkins, appearing in the doorway right on cue. 'Head of history at Ysgol Aneurin.'

'Typical!' cried Ted triumphantly. 'Just typical of Wales!'

'Watch it,' warned Carol. 'Walls have ears.'

'Well, I mean to say . . .'

'Well don't. If it gets about you're anti-Welsh . . .'

'I'm not anti-Welsh, am I? I wouldn't be here if I was.'

'You certainly sounded it. Be more careful, for God's sake.'

Elen had drifted back to her desk. Carol glanced meaningfully at the empty space where she'd been standing, and rolled her eyes.

'So let's get down to business, shall we?' she said coldly.

'What are we talking about?'

'Casting.'

'That's your department, isn't it? Nothing to do with me.'

'I said I'd consult you and that's what I'm doing.' She reeled off a few names. 'They're all more or less confirmed. Though some are a bit iffy.'

'No-one really big, is there?' Ted said dolefully. 'Pity we can't get Ioan Gruffudd.'

'On our budget?' scoffed Carol. 'Give me a break, Ted.'

'He'd be great as Trevor Rowley.'

'I daresay he would. But we've got to be realistic.'

'We might get on network with him.'

'Pigs might fly.'

'That's the trouble with this outfit. The thinking's too small.'

'You didn't say that when I offered you the job,' Carol said sharply. 'You were glad enough to take it then.'

'I know, I know,' he said quickly. 'Don't get me wrong, Carol. But everything could be so much . . .' his fingers fluttered in a swift gesture of frustration, '*bigger.*'

'Don't I know it. But we're stuck with what we've got. And it's a lot better than I thought we'd ever have, so let's be grateful.'

Meekly accepting the reprimand, Ted half listened to his daughter's run-down of potential players. The names she reeled off were all depressingly familiar. Although he was still new to the ways of the media in Wales, it seemed to him that if a bomb dropped on a bus containing a select dozen or so thespians, the entire TV drama output would dry up. As Carol chuntered away, he felt increasingly restless. The story he'd just been reading in the paper rankled. The last thing he wanted was to be a public figure. The Angry Young Man was long buried.

'Well?' said Carol. 'What do you think?'

'About what?'

She sighed. 'You haven't been listening, have you? I wondered if Glyn Pengelly would be right as Dai Sledge.'

Ted wagged his head. 'Don't know about that. Anyone else come to mind?'

Before Carol could answer, Elen stuck her face round the door. 'Someone for you in reception,' she told Ted. 'Name of Kate Dawson.' The face disappeared.

'Who's Kate Dawson?' asked Carol, mystified.

'Haven't got a clue,' he lied. He raised his voice. 'Who is she, Elen?'

Silence. So she *had* taken offence at Ted's 'typical of Wales' comment. Father and daughter exchanged a meaningful look.

'Elen?' Ted repeated.

'She rang you yesterday,' Elen called back from her desk resentfully. 'You asked her round for a coffee.'

'Of course! The cottage woman. I clean forgot.'

'The what?' said Carol.

'Don't look like that. She could be useful.'

'I'm sure she could.'

'I mean as a character. We need someone else, don't we?'

'Is she an actor then?'

'No. I said as a *character*, Carol.'

Carol stared. 'You mean you'd get to know her just to send her up?'

'I might. But she'll need a bit of working on.'

'Well, work away, Ted,' said Carol sarcastically. 'But mind you don't exhaust yourself. You've got a lot of writing to do.'

They sat by themselves at a corner table in a canteen only scantily populated at what, in a less pressurised era, would have been called coffee-time.

'So how are things, OK?' asked Ted, smiling.

'Oh, so-so.' Kate seemed ill at ease, as if regretting she had come. He had forgotten how attractive she was, those clear blue eyes conveying a sense of sexuality and, indeed, recklessness. He felt the beginnings of something perilous and unpredictable, possibly a return to a kind of living he thought he had set aside.

'I'm glad you rang yesterday. I'd been thinking about you,' he lied.

'Had you?'

'Of course. Have you finished that novel I gave you?'

144

'I'm reading it again. I love it.'

'Good.' He gave her one of his warm, intimate looks, feeling he ought to dust it down to make it presentable.

'They're so true to life – your books,' she said impetuously. 'Oh, I *wish* you'd write another.'

'No chance of that,' he said equably. 'I'm too busy.'

'Doing scripts,' she said flatly.

He nodded. 'We're going into production soon. All hell's breaking loose.'

'What's it about, Ted – this thing you're working on?'

'Oh, this and that. Nothing to set the Taff on fire, that's for sure.'

She frowned. 'You mean it's no good?'

'I didn't say that. But no-one will see it outside Wales.'

'Why not, if it's so good?'

'Because that's the way the system works, darling,' replied Ted, risking the jocular endearment. 'The big boys have got the network sewn up. People like Cambrian don't stand a chance.'

'But that's not fair.'

'How long has TV been fair?' How long has *life* been fair, he added inwardly. 'It's the way of the world, Kate.'

She looked thoughtful and dissatisfied. 'So you're taking me to a Hallowe'en Party,' Ted said quickly. 'That's very good of you. Why me?'

'Because Colin's away,' she replied, then looked embarrassed. 'That sounds awful. I didn't mean it like that.' (Pity, he thought instantly.) 'I'd have asked you anyway – everyone's got to bring a surprise guest.'

'So I'm the surprise, am I?'

She nodded. 'It's awfully cheeky of me, I know.'

'I think it's marvellous. I'm very flattered.'

'*They'll* be the ones flattered, Ted.'

'I don't know about that. Who's giving it then – this party?'

'Couple called Collins – Brendan and Sophie. You'll like them,' said Kate, with more conviction than she felt.

'Big friends of yours, are they?'

'I wouldn't say that. Joyce knows them better – my next-door neighbour.'

'Irish, are they?'

'*He* is – sort of. Though I don't know if he was born in Ireland.'

'Not like you.'

'No.'

Sipping his coffee, he looked at her meditatively. 'You're very Irish, aren't you?'

'What do you mean by that?' she asked, more sharply than she intended.

'Your voice. Your manner. You're so . . .'

'So what?'

He risked it. 'So challenging.'

'*Challenging?*'

'Yes. Don't you know that? It's in everything you do.'

'But you hardly know me!'

'I know. Silly, isn't it?'

She fiddled with her cup. 'I don't know how to take that,' she murmured.

'As a compliment. That's the way it's meant.'

There was an awkward pause. Twenty years ago – ten, even – he would have plunged in with a proposition. But now he saw it all in fast-forward – the clinches, the

146

seduction (and who would be the seducer, who the seduced?), the lies, the apprehension, the guilt.

'Anyway,' he said, 'I'll come to the party. If you really want me to.'

'Of course I do.' She looked both disappointed and irritated. 'I've just said so, haven't I?'

The two women looked at him expectantly when he returned to the office. 'Well?' said Carol.

'Well what?'

'Did you set her alight? Will she give her all to you?'

'Do you mind.'

'Not losing your grip, are you?'

Elen flashed nervous glances from daughter to father and back again, not knowing what lay behind this and where it might lead.

'We had a coffee together, that's all. She's very pleasant company.'

'I'm so glad. So we aren't going to make a character out of her after all then, are we?'

'I don't know. We might,' said Ted insouciantly, sprawling with studied ease and plunging into the pages of *The Guardian*.

'Well, let me know in good time, won't you? I'll have to cast her.'

'There's plenty of time, don't worry.'

'Oh! Listen to Mr Laid Back.'

Ted lowered his paper. 'Anything bothering you, Carol?'

'No! Nothing at all.'

'Nobody got back at you about last night since I've been out?'

'No. What makes you think that?'

'I just wondered. You seem all edgy all of a sudden.'

'I'm not edgy. Just busy. I'd like episodes three and four, if you can spare the time.'

Ted glanced at Elen, who was suddenly engrossed in calling up a file on her computer.

'You'll have them by Friday, not before,' said Ted, flinging the paper aside.

'That's good of you,' said Carol dryly. As he reached the door, she added: 'Enjoy the party. Watch out for those witches.' She smiled sweetly.

17

They sat in opposite window seats on the Inter-City, pretending to be at ease with one another. Colin had brought a sturdy leather travelling bag and a smart black briefcase, Yvonne a fawn-coloured suitcase. The suitcase was brand new, though she would not have admitted this to anyone. As the train gathered speed he made a pretence of reading *Time* magazine, but the words were mere shapes, without any meaning. He felt disorientated, as if he did not belong in either the time or the space in which he existed. The image of his father hovered between him and the printed page, a man so remote that he could be imagined only vaguely. He had a voice rather than a shape, a deep voice heard from upstairs as he lay in the front bedroom with his brother sleeping soundly on the upper bunk bed. The voice rumbled on, then stopped, then started again, the only meaning in the sound that it made, the sound that, to the boy he had been, was wordless yet menacing. There was nothing good in that sound. It made him clutch the blankets, pulling them over his head. But one day the sound was no more, and he was alone with his mother and brother.

He turned the page, glanced up, smiled at Yvonne, seeing a reflection of his own nervousness in the tense, shadowed look on her face. And the vagueness that was his father was spirited away, into the nothingness from which it had emerged. Suddenly he felt buoyant, excited, grateful for the good fortune that had led to his being in this train, at that moment, with an attractive woman whose very nervousness proved he meant something to her.

'OK?'

She nodded, looking out at the flat land, intersected by dark lines of ditches, a miniature East Anglia that just (but only just) prevented Cardiff and Newport from having merged into a single city.

He tried again. 'You looking forward to the conference?'

'I don't know.' He hadn't realised till now how dark her eyes were, beneath those bushy brows he did not find at all unattractive. The eyes were not so much brown as blue, but a blue so deep as to be almost a new colour. They stirred him strangely, so that he moved boldly on.

'You'll enjoy it. I know you will. It's so well run. Nobody's allowed to blab on and on. A red light comes on and that's it. Whoever's speaking has to stop.'

The phrase 'red light' made her heart jump.

'But I can't help thinking I don't belong there. Why's he sending me, do you think?'

'To get more experience – that's what he told me. It's bound to benefit you, isn't it? Benefit us all, really.'

'I don't know. It's weird.'

'Not sorry, are you?' The understanding he had thought existed between them seemed threatened, by this unexpected honesty in her manner.

She gave him a long look. The ice broke. 'No,' she said simply. 'I'm not sorry in the least. Fancy a coffee?'

'I certainly do. It's so bloody early.'

'I'll get them.' She sprang to her feet.

'They'll be coming round with a trolley soon.'

'Oh, I can't wait for that. You don't take sugar, do you?'

'No.' They looked at each other mischievously, as if they were compromised ever so slightly.

'Anything to eat?'

'No thanks. Just coffee.'

The elderly man sitting next to Colin rustled his *Times* in what seemed to be a disapproving manner, as if his antennae for scandal had been aroused even by such a brief exchange of words and looks. Colin relaxed, looking comfortably out at the drenched, late-October plain where the gloomy waters of the Severn Sea were kept at bay only by walls and embankments built generations ago. He felt suspended between one phase of his life and another, the old one of unquestioned loyalty to Kate and a new one, existing still merely in chrysalis form, in which Yvonne must somehow play a part. How deep a part he did not yet know; he had no fixed idea of what he wanted from her in London; they might make love and they might not. He was a man in a railway carriage, experiencing single moments in unending procession, each one the only reality, gone as soon as experienced. What was he, the sum of all those moments or something entirely apart, a will-o'-the-wisp without any substance? He waited for Yvonne's return; the man shook his paper irritably; the train rattled on, a succession of steel tubes filled with puzzled, racked humanity.

'Derek! Joyce! How the devil are you? And Kate! Where's Colin?' Brendan raised his arms in a huge gesture of welcome, his florid Punch-like face more roseate than ever. 'He's what? In London? The little devil! What's he getting up to there, don't tell me, I know! . . . Who? . . . Ted Sloane? Never heard of you, but don't worry, I've never heard of anyone, you're very welcome. Pleased to meet you, my good sir,' pumping his hand, 'any friend of Kate and Colin's is a friend of mine. Now come along in and meet everyone.' The pumpkin-hung door was firmly closed, the small party ushered into the warmth and benevolence of a house famous for its hospitality and sheer unexpectedness. Ted, blinking at the brightness of the light and the brassiness of the reception, felt Kate close by his side, felt too the warmth of the support she gave him now as she sensed his alienation and self-doubt. She touched his hand – was that an accident? – then gave it a squeeze, and that was certainly no accident. And then they were all being bundled into a large room filled with weirdly-dressed people, the lights so dim that it was hard to make out exactly what was happening. Names, introductions, all was lost in a swirl of noise and laughter. Ted, clutching a drink that had appeared in his hand as if by magic, found himself hemmed into a corner with a masked woman all in black, who asked him questions he could not properly hear and did not especially wish to answer. 'You're what? . . . What?' she asked urgently, her full, scarlet lips appearing oddly independent of the rest of her face. 'I inspect gas meters,' he bawled, and she collapsed with laughter, bending towards him so that her white breasts, not very well covered up, seemed to glow luminously in the half-light. He had a weird sense of dispossession, as if he had been emptied of himself and filled up by someone he did not know. Her laughter seemed to come from the empty air

152

surrounding her. 'Stop that!' he cried suddenly, 'stop that, do!' and he pushed his way through the crowd none too carefully, evoking a 'Hey, watch it!' from a man who clutched his drink more fervently in the face of this unexpected threat. He felt he must find Kate, to keep some grasp on what was happening. Everyone around him appeared to be in fancy dress, another unsettling phenomenon. His progress was halted absolutely by a witch with straggly grey hair beneath a conical black hat and dense black eyebrows, arched to such a height that they gave her a look of immense surprise. Her long, sharp nose and pale thin lips disturbed him with the ghost of a childish terror, quickly dissipated by the plummy voice issuing from this vision from hell. 'You're Ted, aren't you? Welcome to the party!' He nodded goofily, pressed against her by a surge from behind, a pleasant sensation given that she was obviously possessed of a profoundly unwitchlike body (that's to say, unwitch-like in the terms in which he had hitherto seen witches). 'Oops!' she said delightedly, and he realised (absurd he had not done so before) that the hair was as artificial as the mask. 'I'm Sophie,' she said. 'Sorry about this. We aren't always so crowded. Damn!' The pressure relented and he was able to step back a pace. 'Where's your drink? Have you got a drink?' He made a foolish, empty-handed gesture, in as great a puzzlement as herself, for he could not remember putting it down (where *could* one find an empty space?) or being dispossessed of it. 'Hang on. What would you like? Scotch? You look like a whisky man. Brendan!' she called, over her shoulder. 'Get this man a Scotch. What a bloody awful host you are.' It was only then that he realised, witless as he was, that the witch was his

153

hostess, and immediately he felt comforted, as he had been at a far-distant party when, a small boy amid a swamp of strangers, he had suddenly seen his big sister emerge to pick him up and soothe him with soft words and a smile. Miraculously, they had space to see each other properly and the din appeared to have subsided enough for them to make themselves heard. 'I *do* apologise. Bloody Brendan always goes overboard – invites every-bloody-one within miles – I don't mean you, of course, you're very welcome – you write books, don't you? – can't say I've read any but – oh, piddle!' as a push from her rear squeezed her up against Ted again. He smiled understandingly, seeing her eyes through the mask, large liquid eyes grotesquely at odds with her disguise. 'I didn't know it was fancy dress,' he said, finding his tongue. 'What?' Sophie asked. 'Fancy dress,' repeated Ted. 'Here.' 'It isn't,' replied Sophie. 'Not altogether. It's – shit!' as her glass, knocked sideways, spilt some of its contents over Ted. Brendan, leering magnificently at the sight of Ted and his wife wedged so close, pressed a glass into Ted's hand as the pressure relaxed again and Sophie stepped back. 'Enjoying yourself?' bawled Brendan. Ted nodded. 'Too damn crowded,' Brendan bawled on. 'Never mind. How long've you known Kate and Colin?' Ted shook his head to show he didn't know Colin at all. 'Great couple. Do anything for you, won't they, Soph?' His wife shrugged. 'Come around again. Get to know you properly. Sorry. Circulating, y'know.' Brendan, his crimson Mr Punch face beaming with delight, moved on.

Ted stood hazily, ignored by everyone, his sense of alienation returning. 'Ted,' murmured Kate, sidling up from nowhere, 'I thought I'd lost you. Where the devil did you get?' The gloom, the din, the chaos, absurdly exaggerated the lilt in her voice, as if she were speaking stage Irish. 'God knows,' he replied. 'I don't know where I bloody am.' 'Never mind. Let's get out of here.' She took his arm, steering a way masterfully through the devils and vampires to the door. The hall was now in total darkness, filled with clinching couples. She elbowed her way to the stairs. Ted wondered wildly where she was taking him. Halfway up she plonked herself down and he squatted beside her. 'Christ, what a place!' she exclaimed. 'To think I let you in for all this!' 'That's OK. It's –' Again he stopped. He seemed unable to complete a sentence. 'They're Joyce and Derek's friends really,' Kate went on. 'I can't stand them – well, she's not too bad but Brendan . . .' He tried to say, 'I know what you mean,' but no words came out. 'I'm terrible, aren't I?' she said. 'Talking like this. In their own house.' They were touching, sides, hips, thighs. He pressed his knee hard against hers and she pressed back. Their mouths did not quite meet at first but the second attempt was better. It was he who pulled back first, apologising. 'Don't,' Kate urged. 'Please. There's nothing to be –' And then they were kissing again, as if the world was coming to an end. 'Come upstairs,' he found himself saying, 'come up now, please.' She gasped and shook her head wildly. Wedged together, they kissed until the door to the living-room was flung open and Brendan cried, 'What're you doing out here! Come in, you buggers! Sophie, they're bloody shagging out here. Come and stop them, will you?' The clinching couples loudly denied the charge of copulation. 'Yes you are,' shouted Brendan. 'Don't tell bloody lies!' Kate squeezed Ted's hand and they stood up, he tumescent as a young stag.

Back in the living-room, Brendan took command. 'Now! We're going to play a game. Do you hear me? Listen, you buggers!' Some 'whoo-whoos' of protest, quickly silenced, and an uncanny hush as Brendan began his spiel. 'It's a party game. With a difference. It's got to be different, hasn't it? Because I invented it. And you're all going to play it. Every one of you.' His voice was commanding, somehow richer than usual, and Kate shivered. This wasn't quite right: she knew it. Close beside her, Ted squeezed her hand. She looked up at him gratefully. 'It's a hunting game. OK, OK, I know some of you are against blood sports, but you won't be against this. This is hunting with a difference, because we'll be hunting – the Vixen.' The lights came on suddenly, to gasps and exclamations of surprise. 'I present her to you now – the Vixen!' The apparition stood in the doorway – a tall, slim figure with a fox's head and (so it seemed) a fox's body. She bowed, thin arms raised, spectral-pale. Her nails were long and scarlet, as if dripping blood. Someone shrieked. 'The Vixen,' repeated Brendan in a low voice. 'Do you like her?' A strange murmur swept the room, half protest, half admiration. 'She's different, isn't she? She certainly is different – and she's yours!' Brendan hurled the word at them triumphantly. 'Yes – yours. Because you have to hunt her, all of you! She's going to hide somewhere in the house and you have to hunt her! By touch! That's all you'll have to go on – the feel of her! That fox fur – so smooth, so tasty, so absolutely like nothing you've ever felt before. Isn't that right, Vixen?' The apparition nodded. 'So off with the lights – all of them!' Sudden darkness as the lights were clipped off at the mains. Shrieks and yells, cries of protest mingled with bays of excitement. 'Find her – find her!' shouted

Brendan. 'She'll be in the house somewhere. Not outside, remember – no going in the garden. Inside only – and *she* may be inside something. Boxes, cupboards, beds – she could be anywhere! Just find her, find her!' Kate, to her astonishment, was gripped by fear and excitement. *This is what the witch hunters felt long ago,* she found herself thinking, as people pushed past her, pale faces in the gloom, alien, inescapable. 'Ted – don't leave me!' she gasped. An immediate reply – 'Don't worry – I'm here.' His hand clasping hers tightly, as she struggled to keep her feet against the throng surging to the door. 'I don't want any part of this!' a female voice tremored near her, while others made barely human sounds, those of the mob in pursuit of its quarry. Then Ted's arm around her, holding her firmly, she leaning into him, thinking suddenly of Colin. Feet chumbled upstairs, whoops and screams and a shout of *Tally-ho!* 'Hell's bells,' breathed Ted. 'The man's a maniac.' He grooved a path for them to a corner of the room, miraculously empty. 'Where's Joyce and Derek?' Kate asked in a small, stifled voice. She leaned fully into him, her head on his chest, and his hands began smoothing her back, up and down, round and round. She felt helpless, disorientated, still filled by this strange, wild excitement. She raised her face and he kissed her, and all the passion in her body aroused by this weird, madcap game surged up into her mouth, gathered itself there and merged with the passion passing from his mouth into hers. They were all feeling and touch, their tongues writhing and bodies merging into one as if their clothes were as insubstantial as will o'the wisps. Yet their hands did nothing save embrace one another; their lovemaking was entirely oral, a thing of lips and saliva and tongues. They remained so until a shout of triumph upstairs revealed an end to the game. He wrenched himself away from her just as the lights came on, a rude and arrogant blaze. She pressed her hands to her eyes, her knees almost giving way. His arms went around her again, simply to steady her. And, amid the bawling of Brendan the Vixen was back in the room, minus the fox's head, a white-faced girl with huge eyes and foxy-red hair, smiling crazily and holding aloft the hand of an elderly woman. 'Maggie found me!' she cried. 'Trust a woman to find a woman!' The shouts and cheers made Kate's head swim, and she leaned for support against Ted.

'Who was she?' burbled Joyce afterwards. 'How could she do such a thing?'

'Probably one of the kissogram crowd,' offered Derek, at the wheel of the car sweeping them home through the dull suburban streets. 'They're used to it.'

'But anything could have happened to her – she might have been killed!'

Pity she wasn't, thought Ted. He and Kate sat apart from each other in the back seat, giving nothing away.

Joyce half turned. 'Where did you two get? I hardly saw you.'

'I didn't see you either. Did you join in the chase?' asked Kate.

'I should say – didn't we, darling?' Derek said nothing. 'It's not every day we get a game like that – trust Brendan!'

'Does he always do things like that then?' Kate asked resentfully.

'Yes, I told you – they were part of a wife-swopping crowd back in the Sixties. They've always been swingers,' said Joyce.

That's what they ought to do – swing. Kate kept the thought to herself.

'Didn't you enjoy it then?' Joyce said.

'No. I thought it was ghastly.'

'Ghastly? That's a strong word, Kate.'

'I could find stronger.'

'Hoh! Didn't know you were so prudish . . . What about you, Ted?'

He paused. 'It was different.'

'Well,' said Joyce flatly. 'We shan't take *them* along anywhere again, shall we?'

Derek was silent. He turned off the main road. 'Drop you off first, Ted, shall we?'

'Please.' He was silent, then added: 'Nice of you to take me – I appreciate it.'

'Don't thank us – thank Kate. You're her guest,' said Joyce brusquely. And then, relenting, 'But it's nice meeting you, Ted – I've never met a real live author before. In the flesh, you might say,' she added, almost coyly.

'Nice meeting you too, Joyce,' Ted returned.

'You must come and see us again – mustn't he, Kate? Give him a chance to meet Colin.'

'Mm.'

'I wonder what *he's* up to tonight. Oh, but knowing Colin – he'll be keeping his head down, beavering away at something. Wouldn't you say, Kate?'

'I haven't got a clue.'

The car ground on along the country lane, the four humans in it enveloped in a thick, brooding, impenetrable silence.

Yvonne had feared she might find the conference boring, but in fact she was engaged by it right away. 'We can skip some of the lectures,' Colin had assured her, but they attended most of them, she eager and attentive, he concentrating on her rather than on the words of the speaker. In this new context, she seemed different in a way he could not properly assess: lither, younger even, her whole being alive, lit up by some inner force he had not hitherto suspected. Sometimes she would turn to him, eyes glittering, with a remark both perceptive and unexpected, so that he saw his presence at the conference as subordinate to hers. Over cups of tea mid-afternoon, he said, 'You know, you're wasted as a PA. You ought to be qualified yourself.' 'Oh no, don't be silly!' she replied. 'That would spoil it, don't you see? I'd be like the rest of you then.' And he knew exactly what she meant, the contrast between her enthusiasm and the delegates' questioning, sometimes cynical appraisal of the words from the platform being essentially the difference between the amateur and the professional.

In the evenings they dined together, had drinks in the hotel, then went their separate ways to bed, she to the first floor, he to the second. They were both restrained in a way that had not seemed possible to either, and which came as a relief to them both. He was able to phone Kate, last thing at night, with a clear conscience, and to wake next morning feeling both disappointed and refreshed.

'So you're not back tomorrow?' Kate said on the Friday night.

'No, there's a get-together in the evening. I told you, remember?'

'Right. I might as well go to that Hallowe'en party then.'

'I thought you were going anyway.'

'I am.' The way she put down the phone abruptly rattled him, as if she suspected him of being up to something.

And of course he was. He hadn't told her he was with Yvonne. He had done nothing about it so far. He felt a little foolish.

In that last, Saturday morning session, they were less at ease with one another, both of them aware that a time of decision was approaching. They had one more night together before returning to the ordinariness of their day-to-day living, the sheer weight of habit that would pin them to routines they had only temporarily escaped.

'Feel like doing a show this afternoon?' he asked her at breakfast.

'I don't mind,' she replied. He smiled faintly. 'I mean – yes, I would,' she added awkwardly. 'There *are* matinees, I suppose?'

'Plenty.'

They settled for *Phantom of the Opera*. He booked two seats through his Visa card. They were good seats in the stalls, not too far back: they had struck lucky with returns. A stranger would have noted them as a couple of indeterminate age, dressed in smart casuals, polite and friendly and probably out to make an impression on one other. They ordered drinks for the interval, settled into the dark, enjoyed the show and, increasingly, felt less pressurised by the demands of this final, consuming day. He wondered whether to take her hand, decided against it, felt her nearness as acutely as any physical touch. Afterwards they had a coffee in a nearby café, and it was he who at last voiced the thought that had been occupying both their minds: 'Do you want to go to this party tonight especially?'

'Not particularly.'

They shared the shy smile of accomplices.

'I thought we might have dinner out. Somewhere really nice,' said Colin.

'Suits me.'

'Good. I was hoping you would.'

'Know anywhere nice?'

'One or two.'

He could have taken her to a greasy-spoon transport caff and she'd have been happy. Instead she found herself in Soho, where they went Greek and got a taxi back at midnight.

They had a last liquor in the residents' bar before taking a lift to the first floor, where they both stepped out. Her room was 121. 'Coming in?' she asked.

'Of course.'

It was the little things that surprised him, the particular way she set her make-up on the dressing-table, the fact that she had Lawrence's *Sons and Lovers* on her bedside table. He smoothed her eyebrows with his finger, saying 'Lovely' before kissing her, and she smiled comfortably as if he had said it to her many times before.

They lay naked next to one another, holding hands, their thighs touching. He gloried in the smell of her body, not the perfume she had so delicately applied to it but the body itself, skin and flesh and the layers beneath, the wholesome, mysterious smell that no-one else would have detected because it came to him not through his senses but through his nerves, the sympathy with her that had brought him into this room and into her bed, where he enjoyed her (and she him) as profoundly as if their bodies had been entangled in the act of love.

It was thus that they fell asleep, and woke together, and kissed again, the early-morning staleness spirited away by the mingling of the juices of their mouths and the sudden, riveting excitement. Their first intimacy was quickly over, but followed by something slower in which knowledge played a part, the knowledge that their lives were irredeemably altered.

18

Ffion Tomos had once fancied herself as a poet, reaching the pinnacle of her success by taking second prize in the school eisteddfod for a heartfelt poem on the theme of *Ceremony*. She was sixteen at the time, in the Lower Sixth, and had produced in passable *cynghanedd* a celebration of the ceremony of the seasons, making a slow and stately progress through the year. It would have helped, she realised later, if the theme of nature had been linked in some way with the concerns of humanity, for the first prize had gone to a girl who had written a poem about the three Welsh nationalists who had set fire to an RAF station in the Lleyn peninsula in the 1930s, the ceremony in question being the show trial of the culprits before an English jury. Ffion's disappointment had been keen, but this in itself had not been enough to persuade her to abandon the thorny path of the bard for sweeter pastures; rather was it the sense that her poetic gifts were attuned to a less astringent time than the present, and that rural rhapsodies had a brief shelf life in the thrusting, modern Wales. At university she had discovered, with relief, her ability to coax favours out of people, especially males, and after the torrid romance that had led to the unwanted pregnancy (and fervently wanted abortion), she had acquired self-control, poise, charm and deviousness, all required attributes in the world of public relations in which she operated so successfully.

Although she had long given up writing poetry she still enjoyed reading it, but it was poetry in English that attracted her most, especially when read by the poets themselves. She loved the showiness of performance poets, their absolute commitment to self-aggrandisement, and when the capacity for display was welded to genuine poetic gifts she felt a thrill that was almost erotic. She was almost moved to write fan mail to some of those on the Cardiff circuit, being dissuaded only by the sense that a self-respecting PR should keep a certain distance from those whom she might one day wish to manipulate.

After a particularly lively reading at the Chapter Arts Centre one evening, she was enjoying a drink in the bar when a familiar voice greeted her.

'Ffion Tomos, if I'm not very much mistaken? And all on her own, too? How is that? Are you going into a nunnery, or is it that you just can't stand the blokes any more?'

'Neither,' responded Ffion coolly, looking up into the blandly smiling face of Conrad Matthews, Press Officer of Cambrian Television. 'I just like my own company.'

'Very sensible. Wish I could say the same thing myself.' For a second a bitter truth showed itself in the inflexion in Conrad's speech, the sudden set of his face, but it vanished as quickly as it came and he was once again the boisterous PR exuding phoney bonhomie. 'Well, what are you doing here, may I ask? Meeting someone, or may I join you?'

'By all means.' She nodded at the vacant chair opposite and Conrad plonked himself heavily upon it, spilling a thin trickle of ale down the side of his recharged glass. 'I've been to the poetry reading, if you must know.'

'God! The Cardiff poets!' groaned Conrad, theatrically grimacing. 'All gas and no gaiters,' he added obscurely.

'I like them. They're sparky.'

'Well, Ffion *bach*, it takes all sorts. How's business then? Still shooting the PR rapids?' He smiled hugely, revealing white, expensively-bridged teeth that Ffion found especially repulsive.

'What the hell do you mean by that, Con? Talk English, for God's sake.'

'To you? A product of Ysgol Gyfun Rhisiart? It's more than my life's worth.'

'Come off it, Con. You're not talking to Merched y Wawr now.'

A sharp, explosive laugh served as a punctuation mark between Conrad's public persona and the private one he assumed instantly. His physical shape seemed to alter, becoming more tucked-in, his face leaner and more sharply defined.

'It's a bugger, Ffion,' he said in a low voice.

'What, Con?'

'Everything.'

'The job?'

'Partly.'

She let a few moments pass.

'And Sandy?'

'Don't ask.'

'OK.' She paused. 'I'm sorry, Con.'

He smiled bleakly. 'It'll all come out in the wash, I expect. And me with it.'

She lowered her eyes, then looked up and smiled. 'Anyway, how's the new project coming along?'

'Which one?'

'Is there more than one? You surprise me.'

'You mean *Rowley's Patch?* Oh, sorry – I mean *Punters.*'

'Is that what it's called now?'

He nodded. 'Worse luck. Bloody silly idea.'

'Oh, why?'

'Well, it's been used before, hasn't it? Not that that lot would know.'

'Don't think much of them, do you?'

'Much of them? *Iffern.* I think as much of them as two ducks shagging a lettuce.'

Ffion's bright ring of laughter caused some twisting of heads; it was an unexpected sound.

'So whose idea was it? Changing the title?'

'Who do you think? Ted Sloane. The Angry Young Man. Jesus.'

'Really?' The faintest pink, undetected by Conrad, stained the underside of the skin on Ffion's pale cheek.

'You saw him being taken apart by Jasper Taylor, didn't you? *Iesu Grist.* It's a wonder he could show his face in public after that.'

'On Jasper's show then, was he?'

'No – Rupert Fallon was. Bloody hell, Ffion, where've you been, girl? You're slipping. Jasper gave him a right old going-over. Talked about the Taffia still running things in Wales. All a load of dog's manure of course, but he made Rupert squirm, I can tell you. Ted Sloane too, I'll be bound.'

'Because of Carol Hart, you mean?'

'Of course. What else? Father and daughter – nepotism rules. Hey – you didn't have a hand in it, did you?'

'Why me?' Ffion looked pained. 'I don't know a thing about it.'

'Now that *does* surprise me – with all your contacts.'

167

He gave her a keen look which she rode with consummate ease. 'Thought Gwynne Tecwyn might have mentioned it,' he added, with a poor attempt at carelessness.

'And why should he?' asked Ffion, suddenly the Ice Maiden.

'Well – seeing he's involved . . .' returned Conrad uncomfortably.

'Not with me, he isn't.'

'Oh – I'm sorry.'

'That's quite all right, Conrad. Just not up to date, are you? Bad as me. Now you can get me a vodka and tonic, please.' She glittered him a forgiving smile.

He came back bowing and scraping like a penitent. Normal service was resumed.

'There's something I've been meaning to ask you,' he said, having just thought of it. 'Are you very busy these days?'

'Desperately.'

'Oh, there's a pity. I was hoping you might do a job for me.'

'I might. Try me.'

He gave her an odd look. 'It concerns Ted Sloane, as a matter of fact.'

'Oh yes?'

'Do you feel like interviewing him? He's a very interesting man.'

'I'm sure he is. But why me?'

'I don't want to do it myself. You'd make a much better job of it.'

'Don't give me crap, Con. What've you got in mind, exactly?'

'A feature. On him. Personality piece. Full of colour. You know the sort of thing. Something I can send round all the papers. Angry Young Man makes a come-back. Just up your street, I reckon.'

'Hasn't anybody done it yet?'

'No. Surprising, isn't it? Shows how long he's been dead. Who cares about Angry Young Men now?'

Ffion gave him a long look. 'What makes you think they'll care if I do it?'

'I think they will. Probably send their own people down, mind – but it'll hook 'em.'

'I'm not so sure of that. I'll think about it.'

'No. I've got to know now, Ffion. I'll pay you well – don't worry.'

'You'd have to. What about him, though – will he play ball?'

'He will now. After all this kefuffle.' Conrad smiled maliciously. 'Owes us one, doesn't he?'

Kate was suspicious of Colin's attentiveness. He had come back from the conference in a mellow mood, full of solicitousness and deeply interested in the Hallowe'en party he had missed. She gave him the minimum of information, mentioning the masks and the witches but not the Vixen or Ted. She was pretty sure he'd been with Sharon but any mention of her name brought only a steady look and not even the faintest emanation of guilt. Kate trusted her own ability for reading signs, feeling vibrations and so on, but her antennae picked up nothing. Could it be that Colin was still what he had always been, the monstrously perfect husband? It had all happened so quickly, the way her irritation with his overweening patience and understanding had given way to the shifting sands of suspicion, that she felt distrustful of everything –

herself included. What had Ted meant by those kisses? Anything or nothing? The days following the party were full of a wild expectation that he might call in to the shop and invite her out, or – more romantically – press a note into her hand, or even ring her at home – but how would he know her number? Several times she picked up the phone and stared at it, daring herself to call him at the studios – but how could she know he was there? And even if he were, what could she say to him? She knew exactly how that woman in his office – the one she'd spoken to before – would sound when she asked for him – polite on the surface, amused and contemptuous beneath. No, she couldn't face it! So, distracted by her suspicions of Colin and uncertainty over Ted, she sought diversion in her stints at the charity shop. She was doing three half days now, plus a whole day on Thursday, much to Jill's delight and Pam's amusement. 'What's up with you, dalling? Bored or something?' 'No more than you,' Kate retorted, but soon learned that Pam had an answer to everything. 'No answer to that, honey. I'm as bored as a eunuch in a brothel.' Her private life was a mystery to Kate: twice divorced, with no steady partner apparently, Pam gave nothing away about her sex life. 'You could be earning good money somewhere,' Pam chided her. 'What's the point of doing this charity crap?' 'The same goes for you. Why do you do it?' 'Passage to heaven, dalling. Sins to be forgiven.' It was a relationship that assumed great importance for Kate, as she fought to keep a foothold in her slippery-sliding world. She knew she could never be close friends with Pam but her company was a boon, her insouciance a welcome distraction.

It was Jill's absence for a day that brought the two

women closer together. They were sorting through two huge trunks of mainly garbage in the back room with Sylvia (a once-willowy blonde who boasted of being a former Tiller girl) serving in the shop, when Pam asked, out of the blue, 'How's your writer friend getting on these days, dalling?' Kate's cheeks felt hot as she replied swiftly, 'He's not my friend. I hardly know him.' 'But he gave you a book of his, dalling – he must like you.' Kate, diving into a rag-bag collection of T-shirts and socks, was glad she had not mentioned the party to Pam. 'You can't let it drop,' said Pam directly. 'You've got to do something.'

'What?' asked Kate, throwing the useless junk aside.

'Well – go and call on him.'

'I can't do that!'

'Why not? You know where he lives, don't you?'

'That's the most ridiculous idea I've ever heard in my life,' said Kate heatedly.

'So you're going to do it then, are you?' teased Pam.

'No. I certainly am not.'

Pam, smirking, dropped the subject, only to return to it after Sylvia had left on the heels of a huffy remark about 'doing all the sodding work round here.'

'Kate, dalling, I don't want to interfere but I think Ted Sloane needs a bit of encouragement.'

'Do you?' returned Kate politely, her face registering surprise that Pam had remembered the author's name.

'I certainly do. You owe it to yourself.'

'To myself?'

'Of course. You're not very happy these days, are you?'

'What makes you say that?'

'Kate, love.' Pam's voice, lacking its customary edge of banter, was softer and quieter. 'You can't fool me, whoever else you can fool. Colin's having an affair, isn't he? It's written all over you. Well, don't let it get you down, honey. Carry on living.'

'And have an affair myself, you mean?'

'Did I say that? I wouldn't presume. But do something. Anything.'

Kate, torn between resentment and acceptance, loosely tied a yellow scarf around her neck, put on her coat.

'You know where he lives, don't you?' persisted Pam. 'He's asked you in before. Call and see him.'

'Maybe you should go yourself.'

'Maybe I will at that,' Pam said sweetly. 'I'll eat him up and leave you the leftovers.'

Outside, she added: 'Not cross, dalling? Only trying to help.'

'I know,' Kate acknowledged. 'Thanks, Pam.'

She waved as Pam drove away, then walked briskly home.

'Who the hell's Ffion Tomos? Any relation to Ffion Hague?' asked Ted.

'Not that I know,' answered Carol. 'Why should she be? You're not related to all the Teds in the world, are you? She's a media person. Got her own PR firm.'

Ted grunted. He didn't like talking shop with his daughter on his home patch. He thought she was abusing her position; social calls should be exactly that.

'Anyway, here's a present for you.'

'What's this?' he asked suspiciously.

'Open it and you'll see.'

He took the sweater from the bag, held it at arm's length.

'What's this in aid of?'

'I'm sick of that grubby old jumper you've been wearing. It makes my office look untidy.'

'Oh, I'm sorry about that.' He put the sweater over the arm of the chair next to his. 'You sound just like your mother.'

'Good. I take that as a compliment.' She looked at him keenly. 'Don't tell me you're offended. I thought you might like it.'

'It's all right,' he said diffidently. 'I might wear it now and then.'

'Good.' She smiled. 'I think we ought to go for this, you know, Ted.'

'Do you now.'

'Yes. She'll do a good piece, I know. Just the sort of thing we need.'

'I can't stand PR,' said Ted moodily. 'It's a load of shit.'

'But useful, Ted. Very.'

He looked across the room at his daughter. Jane, his first wife, smiled back at him briefly; then she was gone, her ghost subsumed into the flesh and blood of Carol.

'All right, then,' he said unexpectedly. 'I'll do it.'

He almost regretted his words the moment they were spoken; but not quite.

19

Sir Charles Lewis, head of the Charles Lewis Partnership, did not have a deep love of literature, but he enjoyed what he called 'a good yarn.' And the best yarns, in his opinion, were written by C S Forester, author of the Hornblower novels. They were full of brisk characterisation; peppery action; and they wasted little time in introspection. In his spacious Sixties house in the semi-rural suburb of Lisvane, a house designed, naturally, by himself, he sat immersed in a jaunty tale, chuckling to himself from time to time as Celia, his wife of thirty-five years, placidly embroidered a cushion cover for her niece, Linsey, who was the nearest thing to a child of her own that she would ever possess.

Lady Lewis cleared her throat, a sound so unobtrusive that it would scarcely have registered on the scale of decibels, and murmured, 'Charles, dear, have you decided about Christmas yet?'

Sir Charles grunted.

'Have you, dear?' Celia persisted.

The fact that she had spoken, if not her actual words, penetrated the outer layers of her husband's consciousness. He offered her a blank look.

'Christmas, Charles. What are we doing for Christmas?'

A twinge of irritation creased Sir Charles's forehead. 'What do you want to do?'

'You decide, dear. You always do,' said Celia pacifically.

Sir Charles, comfortably seated beneath a reproduction of Turner's *The Fighting Temeraire*, gave her a long, lingering, knowing look which she ignored completely.

'I don't think that's quite true, Celia. I thought we made a joint decision, with the balance tilted appreciably in your favour.'

'Charles! How could you. It's not like that at all and you know it. I was thinking about Scotland myself.'

Sir Charles frowned. 'Scotland? Why Scotland?'

'Well, that invitation from the Bryans. You know.'

'God, I'd forgotten about that.' He peered over the top of his glasses. 'Are you serious?'

'Of course. Aren't I always?' she asked skittishly.

'No. You know very well you're not,' said Sir Charles, looking very pleased with her skittishness. 'In fact you're the most unserious person I know.'

'And don't you love it!'

'It depends. At the moment I'm not sure. It will be bloody cold up there.'

'Not in the house, Charles. We don't intend climbing Ben Nevis, do we?'

'I certainly don't, I don't know about you. Anyway Ben Nevis is miles away from Edinburgh.'

'Well then. That's all right then, isn't it?'

'No, it certainly isn't all right!' exploded Sir Charles, loving every minute of this. 'Why do you propose to drag me all the way to Scotland when we can have a perfectly good time here on our own?'

'Because it would be fun.'

'Which it wouldn't be with me here, I suppose.'

'Oh, don't be difficult, darling. The Bryans are very

175

nice, and this is the third time they've asked us up there, and if we turn them down this time they'll never ask us again.'

'Well? If we don't want to go there what's the problem?'

'But we do want to go there. Don't we?'

'*You* do.'

'And you do too. You *know* you do, *cariad*.'

The use of the Welsh endearment told Sir Charles that this was serious stuff. 'I can't spare the time.'

'Nonsense! It's Christmas.'

'I'm not quite sure how I'd get on with Alec. After all this time.'

Celia, certain now of her triumph, gave her husband an indulgent look.

'You've always got on well with him perfectly well before. Why should it be any different?'

'Water under the bridge. It's years since we've seen him.'

'Not all that long. Two years last Easter.'

'Long enough. And he's got a new wife.'

'A very nice one too, by all accounts.'

'Much younger than him.'

'You don't disapprove of that, surely?'

Sir Charles met his wife's ironical glance unflinchingly. 'I don't envy him in the least, if that's what you're thinking.'

'Did I say you did?'

A comfortable silence enclosed them. Sir Charles, his attention diverted from Hornblower's exploits, looked pensively at his wife. 'We've been together a long time, haven't we?'

'You could say that.'

'Thirty-odd years.'

'Thirty-five,' Celia corrected.

'Mm. I wouldn't have changed them for anything. In points of detail, perhaps, but nothing major.'

'I'm glad to hear it,' his wife returned ironically. She jabbed in her needle with extra precision. 'What's brought this on exactly?'

'Oh, I don't know . . . I was thinking maybe we could see more of each other.'

'That would be nice, dear.'

'I'm seriously thinking about it, you know. Retirement.'

She gave him a shrewd look. 'Are you?'

'Yes. I think I've had enough. Now would be a good time. To get out.'

'You'd have to be absolutely certain,' she said in a matter-of-fact way. 'There'd be no going back once you've done it.'

'I know.'

She looked at him coolly. 'Who would take over the business?'

'I don't know. I could just sell it.'

'And what about Colin? And Matthew? And the rest of your staff?'

If Sir Charles had been a shrugging man, he would have shrugged.

'They could be out on their noses.'

'They could be,' he agreed.

'You wouldn't like that, would you?'

Sir Charles made a swift, irritable gesture. 'Hang it all, Celia. You don't want me to hang on there till I die, do you?'

'Of course not, darling. But couldn't something be arranged? What do you call it – a buy-out?'

'It might be possible. But I don't know if they can

raise the wherewithal. I'm not going to give it away,' he said spiritedly.

'Of course you're not. But you can start talking to them about it – can't you? If you're serious?'

'Yes. I suppose I can'

He looked at her with respect; even after thirty-five years she was capable of surprising him.

Ffion prepared herself carefully for meeting Ted. She hesitated between a black skirt suit with a zipped jacket – not too formal, she thought – and a choice of two trouser suits, one sky-blue, the other stone. The long coat jacket of the sky-blue outfit told against it in the end: it had an element of fussiness not at all appropriate. She was on the point of plumping for the stone trouser suit – a navy-blue top would go well with it – when she suddenly remembered a jacket and dress with ultra-thin stripes she had worn only once. It was odd, since she had gone off it a bit, for no particular reason; now, however, she took it out, held it against herself as she stared challengingly into her bedroom mirror, and with an inexplicable sense of exhilaration put it on.

Their meeting was timed for three-thirty, the dead centre of the afternoon when Ted Sloane could not write, could not do anything. He was sorry now he had agreed to the interview, but not sorry enough to call it off. A part of him, deep down and mystifying, wanted to go through with it, to see what might follow. Would the nationals be interested in Ted Sloane again? Was he about to do a Lazarus? He'd been big news once, one of the Angries on black-and-white telly, questioned amiably by Cliff Michelmore and with arch knowingness by Huw Wheldon. After the novels dried up he was news of a kind as Francis Kent, TV scriptwriter. They'd had a bit of fun with him – failed Angry dredging up a new career on the box – but soon tired. Who'd be interested now? Angry Young Men were as passé as brown Windsor soup and teddy boy gear. But it might be fun to find out; and anyway he'd enjoy teasing this Ffion woman a little.

He was unexpectedly jumpy during the morning of her visit; he was up to speed with the scripts for *Punters* and was working on some prose which might, just might, prove the basis of a novel. Would he dare to bring it out if he actually finished it? If so, under what name? He wrote a short, fidgety paragraph on his Amstrad, wiped it out, tried again. And then gave it up, taking Trinder for a walk through the drizzle.

He saw her car pull up, moved swiftly from the window. After she rang the bell, he waited long enough for her to contemplate ringing it again before he went to the door. He almost stepped back a pace, surprised by her appearance. The wide-apart hazel eyes, the full lips, the ash-blonde hair, centrally parted and tucked behind her small, shapely ears; he had not expected anything quite like this. 'Mr Sloane?' she said brightly. 'Ffion Tomos.' She held out a cool white hand, which he tentatively grasped as he ushered her in. He felt gauche, shedding fifty years in an instant, to be filled with adolescent uncertainty again.

'Please sit down.' He waved a hand, was fixated by the shine of her hair, the sheer brightness of her. She sat on the settee sideways on to the window, he in the old armchair with scratched legs that had once belonged to his grandfather. The morning drizzle had given way to a clear afternoon, what was left of the daylight highlighting the left side of her face and leaving the other in shadow.

'Fancy a tea? Coffee?' he asked.

'No thanks. But don't let me stop you,' she smiled.

He shook his head, began making conversation, falling easily into old habits after the initial surprise, small talk coming to him as readily as smiles to celebs. She was at ease with him, appreciating the laid-back mastery of it all, the slight pause before the appropriate phrase, the warmth of his smile. Old fraud he might be, but how welcome after the peasant nastiness of Gwynne Tecwyn! As she slowly crossed her legs, noting the appreciative glance this elicited from Ted Sloane, she congratulated herself on her choice of skirt and jacket rather than trouser suit.

It was some time before she eased herself into the real business of the day. 'So what made you come to live in Cardiff, Mr Sloane? You could have written the scripts anywhere, surely?'

'Oh, please – Ted. Don't be formal.' A smile rewarded him. 'I wanted to be close to the action. And I've always liked Cardiff. I've got family connections here, didn't you know? There's no reason why you should, of course.' And to her great surprise (for she had expected some resistance), he gave her the whole shoot – tales of his athlete grandfather, how he'd started writing, even how he'd dug up that old pop bottle in the garden. It all went on the tape he knew was capturing every syllable, for she'd brought out the tiny recorder and placed it on the coffee table between them, but he was hers for the taking, he wanted to hold nothing back from this woman. He told her about his wives, Jane and Letty – two marriages, two divorces – his early fame and disillusion, the lean years scrabbling out a living writing school textbooks, brochures, press releases, hack stuff of the most dreadful kind, then the new career as the TV scriptwriter, Francis Kent, followed by more lean years until now.

'But forgive me, Ted – I must ask you this – isn't it a bit awkward – working for your daughter?'

He frowned, barely perceptibly. 'It is a bit. But we rub along. I do what she asks. I've got no false pride any more.'

'You leave yourself exposed though, don't you – to certain accusations?' The lilting way she pronounced the word 'accusations' delighted him.

'Of nepotism, you mean? I don't give a shit – if you'll excuse me. She chose me because I can do the job. I was only going to be a kind of consultant, you know – but they had some dreadful prat doing the scripting. A complete asshole. So I took over.'

She did not conceal her smile, but he failed to appreciate its full import.

'Yes, I know the man – I'm inclined to agree with you,' she murmured. 'I'm sure you're making a much better job of it. But your novels, Ted – aren't you going to get back to them?'

'I might and I might not. If it happens, it happens. I'm not worried unduly.'

'You'd *like* to be writing them again though, would you? What would they be about, do you think?'

'God knows. I'm not even thinking of it.'

'Wales perhaps? Cardiff?'

'Possibly. We'll wait and see, shall we?'

An edginess in his voice warned her off. She'd got more than she needed to write a piece for Conrad Matthews, and far more than she'd expected.

'And now a drink – yes?' He sprang to his feet,

clapped his hands, an emphatic full stop to the interview. 'I've got some lovely Australian red – do you fancy a glass?'

'I'm driving, remember.'

'Just a glass?'

'Well. Perhaps I will,' she conceded, smiling.

She switched off the recorder, put it into her large leather bag. Her eyes swept the room as he saw to the drinks, noting the miner's lamp in the alcove – a replica, she spotted instantly, not the genuine article – the wood-burning stove, the set of Chinese willow-pattern plates on the old Welsh dresser. A bit of a poseur, certainly – but something nice about him. That strong face and large head – she liked large male heads placed firmly on broad shoulders – the grizzled hair, the large hands, the expressive voice and the charm. Oh yes, he had charm all right. She wouldn't trust him far, but who the hell *would* she trust? As he handed her the glass their fingers touched, not entirely by accident.

It was the thin, watery light of the setting sun, a pale yellow band on the horizon glimpsed between houses in Lavernock Avenue on her way home, that persuaded Kate to change direction and walk, with mounting excitement and apprehension, along the lane leading to the cottage. Colin had a client's meeting which would keep him late at work; it had been a dull day at the shop, in the absence of Pam, and she did not relish being alone in an empty house for two or three hours. A restlessness possessed her these days: she wanted to get away from Cardiff, get away from Colin, who was making a fool of her. That bloody Sharon! She knew he was having an affair with her; she *knew* it.

182

The parked car outside the cottage took her by surprise. She knew it could not be his because he did not possess a car. Could it be his daughter's? It was smart enough to belong to someone in telly. Would it be a social call, or business? Was it hers anyway? She slowed down, undecided, then thought 'To hell with it. I'll call on him anyway.' She walked determinedly up the path, rang the bell. When he opened the door she knew at once that she'd made a mistake, but it was too late now.

'I was just passing, Ted. If it's awkward –'

'Not at all,' he lied. 'Come on in.'

The door closed behind her, a barrier shutting off retreat. The sound reverberated in her head, a dire warning.

'Actually I've just been interviewed, but it's over now,' he smiled.

'Oh, I'm sorry – I didn't know you had company.'

She was in the living-room now, being introduced to a smart woman who looked a million dollars and had more composure in her knuckles than she had in her entire body. Kate felt stupid, flustered, wanted nothing more than to get the hell out of it.

They were both attentive, civilised; it was impossible simply to flee. She sat, accepted a glass of red wine, tried hard to say things that made sense.

'Kate and I were at a wild party the other day – weren't we, Kate? My God, I've never seen anything quite like it.'

'Why, what happened?' Ffion's hazel eyes grew large.

'Everything. The lights went out and we were asked to join in a hunt.'

'A *hunt*? On horseback?'

'No – this was in a *house*, Ffion,' said Ted. 'Someone

dressed up as a fox and we all had to chase around trying to find her.'

'My goodness – it sounds like a real orgy. What happened when you caught her?'

'Oh, nothing. That was the disappointment, I suppose. We just let her go – didn't we, Kate?'

'I'm afraid so. She was called the Vixen,' Kate volunteered, embarrassed.

'The *Vixen*. Highly dangerous,' murmured Ffion, giving Kate an acute look.

Kate, uncomfortable under her scrutiny, burst out with, 'I was glad to get away. I didn't enjoy it very much.'

'Oh, didn't you?' asked Ted, surprised.

Thinking of the way he had deep-kissed her, Kate coloured. Ffion's glance veered swiftly from her to Ted and back again. 'Well,' Ffion said softly, 'so long as no damage was done.'

'It was all in good part. Not a blood sport in the least,' said Ted confidently, giving Ffion a straight look in return.

Kate, sensing the high charge of sexuality behind the apparently straightforward words, felt excluded and angry. He was putting her down, not obviously, but by implication. 'I must be going,' she said, as soon as she could decently leave.

Ted's half-hearted attempts to detain her served only to stoke up her self-loathing. What on earth had possessed her to come around here? How could she possibly imagine he had the least interest in her?

'I'll see myself out, don't worry,' said Kate shortly, but he escorted her to the door.

'You will come again, won't you?' pleaded Ted. 'I'm sorry, I'm a bit tied up now.'

It was on the tip of Kate's tongue to say, 'You may be a lot more tied up soon,' but who was she to suggest that these two were already into bondage? Instead she made do with, 'I didn't know you were busy. I wouldn't have troubled you if I'd known.'

'It's no trouble, I assure you,' he began, but she was already out of the house and stepping briskly down the path.

'Cheers for now,' he called after her hopefully.

'Goodbye,' she returned, not looking back.

Back in the living-room, Ffion was staring down at her glass.

'Well!' he said bluffly. 'Another drink?'

'I'd better not.' She looked up. 'Did I say something wrong?'

'Of course not. Why do you ask?'

'She seemed a bit put out about something.'

'Oh! I wouldn't have said so. I hardly know her really,' Ted bumbled on. 'Her husband's an architect.'

'Was he at the party too?' she asked dryly.

'What? Oh – no. He was away. On business. They nearly bought this place, you know.'

'Oh? And why didn't they?'

'They thought it would cost too much – to put right.'

She smiled. 'Lucky for you then, wasn't it?'

'I should say.'

Ffion's ironical manner was playing havoc with him.

'Would you like to look around? It's quite an interesting old place.'

'Not just now. I must fly. Some other time, maybe.' She stood up, with a disturbing rustle of her dress. 'Well – thanks for your help. I've enjoyed talking to you.'

'My pleasure. Remind me – who are you writing this piece for?'

'Everyone really. Didn't I tell you? It's a job for Cambrian's press office. They'll farm it out round all the papers, I suppose. Just general publicity.'

'So it might be binned all round?'

'It might. But I hope not,' she replied coolly. 'Well, thanks very much.' She put out her hand. 'It's been nice meeting you.'

'You too.' He held her hand a tad longer than necessary. 'See you soon, I hope.'

'You never know.'

She was on her way out.

'Couldn't send me a copy of your piece, could you? I wouldn't like to miss it.'

She met his smile with a steady look. 'Of course. Let me know what you think.'

'OK then.'

'Well,' he said quietly after she'd gone. 'What d'you think of that then, eh?'

Trinder snuggled up to him, in fawning admiration.

20

'I think Colin's having an affair,' said Joyce.

Derek, reading a John Grisham novel, took his time before replying, 'What makes you say that?'

'Because he looks guilty. It's written all over him.'

'How can you say that? We don't see him very often. Unless you see more of him than I do,' he added pointedly.

'He's not having an affair with *me*, if that's what you're thinking. Though I wouldn't mind,' she added pensively, zapping from an old *Rising Damp* on Sky Gold to *University Challenge* and back again. 'I can do with a bit of excitement.'

'Don't let me stop you,' said Derek, turning a page.

'You wouldn't care a bit, would you?'

'If it turns you on . . .'

'Colin doesn't turn me on, I can tell you that for starters. He's too goody-goody.'

Derek looked up at last. 'How can he be goody-goody if he's having an affair?'

'Because he's been driven to it. She doesn't deserve him.'

'Who?'

'Kate of course – who d'you think?'

'I don't know. You might have been talking about the other woman.'

He returned to John Grisham. On the screen, Miss

187

Jones easily deflected Rigsby's pathetic attempts at seduction.

Joyce sighed. 'You're impossible, Derek.'

A burst of studio laughter distracted her. 'Oh, that sounds so false! Do you think it's canned, Derek?'

'I haven't the faintest idea.'

'I think it is. *Definitely*,' she added, after a louder and more sustained corporate laugh. 'I know who he's having it with too . . . Derek! Are you listening?'

Derek carefully put his opened book down, covers up, on his lap. 'I don't have much choice, do I?'

'Well, are you going to ask me who?'

'All right then. Who?'

'Sharon.'

'Who the hell's Sharon?'

'A girl he works with. Kate told me.'

'Well. That's all right then, isn't it?'

He picked up his book again.

'What do you mean, that's all right then?' said Joyce indignantly.

'Well, people are always having office romances. They don't mean anything.'

'Oh, don't they. I hope that doesn't mean *you're* having one.'

'I don't have an office, do I?'

'As good as. There's that girl you're with all day . . .'

'Don't be silly, Joyce.'

'Well, how do I know what you get up to?'

'I assure you, darling, that a dental surgery is *not* the kind of place where romance flourishes.'

'That's what you say,' said Joyce darkly.

'And anyway, I don't fancy her.'

'Bet you do. She's got lovely boobs.'

'Has she? I hadn't noticed.'

'Liar.'

Joyce zapped the set off completely. 'Do you think he is, Derek?' she asked, with a worried look.

'I don't know. You just told me he was.'

'It's only what Kate thinks. I don't know.'

'What's she doing about it?'

'Nothing. She isn't sure.'

Derek looked at his wife. 'I'd be surprised if he is. Wouldn't you? He's such a decent chap.'

'H'm! He's a man, isn't he.'

'Thank you very much.'

Joyce, deep in thought, said nothing.

He undressed her slowly. He was long out of practice, having trouble unclipping her bra. She made a small, admonishing sound, and did it herself. Unclothed, they held each other a long time before getting into bed. He was afraid he might slacken but he remained strong for her. It was quickly over.

Afterwards they lay a long time side by side, holding hands. He turned his head to her. She looked at him steadily.

'Why?' he said.

'Because,' she replied.

He started to caress her again but she said, 'Ssh. Not now.' She stroked his head tenderly.

When she sat up at last, on the edge of the bed, he was amazed by the length of her back, the lovely curve of her spine. He traced it with his finger.

'I'm sixty-three,' he said.

'I don't believe it.'

'I don't either. I don't believe anything.'

'Neither do I.'

189

When she went to the bathroom he stared at the place where she had been. The street lamps of Hollybush glowed orange in the distance.

He hardly moved till she returned.

'You going to stay there all night?' she teased.

'Maybe. Nothing to get up for now, is there?'

'Tch! Don't talk like that. You have to see me off, don't you? I might steal the family silver.'

'That won't get you very far.'

Downstairs, she did not linger.

'When shall I see you again?' he asked.

'Do you want to?'

'Of course I want to.'

She pondered. 'I'll give you a ring.'

Ted read back what he had written on the screen. Should he save this piece of wishful thinking, or simply delete it? He rested his elbows on the arms of his chair and pressed his fingers to his brow, eyes shut. If only it had worked out like that, right away!

He opened his eyes. The words were still there, but now they did not seem to mock him. He smiled faintly, pressed 'Finish Edit' to save the document, and switched off the faithful old Amstrad.

When Colin got back from the meeting he found the house in darkness. He thought Kate might be out but her car was parked in its usual place at the roadside, leaving the drive free for him.

He let himself in, called 'Kate? Kate?'

He switched on the lights in the hall and the living-room. He looked for a note in the usual place, but there was none.

'Kate!' he called again with sudden fear. 'Where are you? Kate?'

He pounded up the stairs, went into their bedroom. A shape was huddled on the bed. 'Kate! Are you all right?'

He leaned over her. She was crying, her head turned away from him.

'What's wrong, love? Tell me!'

She wriggled away from him.

'What is it, Kate?' he said urgently.

'Go away, Colin. *Go away!*'

'But why? What have I done?'

'Christ. You don't have to ask, do you?'

She sobbed, her face pressed into the pillow. With the flat of her hands she beat down upon the bed, over and over.

He stood helplessly, not believing this was happening. He thought back to the morning; all had seemed perfectly normal.

There was Yvonne, of course; but what did she know of Yvonne?

Suddenly, amazingly, he was filled with a sense of relief. He had reached it at last; the moment when his life stood at the point of balance. It could go either way; he was absolved of any decision.

He would play his part to perfection; as he had been playing it, so it seemed, ever since he had been conscious of himself as a living, sensate being.

He sat on the bed, touched the back of her head lightly. She whirled around, struck his hand away.

'Don't you dare touch me! Who the hell do you think you are?'

'If you told me what was wrong, Kate –'

'You know what's wrong! You and that woman!'

'What woman?'

'Sharon of course – who else?'

'Sharon! Did you say *Sharon?*'

'Yes! What's so funny?'

'Sharon,' he cried, shaking. 'Bloody hell.'

'I don't see the joke. What's the bloody joke?' she screamed.

'You must be . . .' He shook with hysterical laughter.

She pushed him with all her might, with both hands. He fell to the floor, doubled up.

'Get out!' she cried. 'Get out of this house!'

He shook his head, convulsed. She kicked him with her bare feet, on his head, his back, his shoulders. He covered his head with his arms as she shouted, 'Go! Now! This minute!'

He got to his feet, his laughter subsiding into long, painful gasps.

'You've got it wrong, Kate. It's – not –'

'What?'

He shook his head feebly.

'Sharon,' he said disbelievingly. 'For Christ's sake, Kate.'

She stood her ground, staring at him. 'Who is it then?'

'Yvonne.'

For a moment there was silence. *'Yvonne,'* she breathed. 'That –'

'Don't, Kate,' he said warningly.

She sprung at him, her hands on his throat. He fought against her, choking. 'You bastard!' she cried. 'Bastard!'

He punched her hard in the chest. She gasped, winded.

He ran down the stairs and out of the house.

Next door, Joyce heard the car that had lately drawn up speed away again, far quicker than it had come. She gave Derek a knowing look.

'You've what?' said Yvonne drowsily, woken up by the phone. She stiffened, taking in what he was saying. '*Left* her. What do you mean? Where are you? . . . The *office*. What the hell are you doing there?' Listening, she ran her free hand over her face. 'God, Colin. You can't do that. How long have you been there? What? You don't know? . . . Listen now, Colin. You can't stay there. You really can't. I'll be down there in a minute . . . Yes I can. Of course I can. Just stay where you are. And don't worry.' She slammed down the phone. 'Jesus. *Jesus*.'

She sprang out of bed, flung some clothes on, dabbed on some make-up. 'Twenty past twelve,' she said out loud. 'What a bloody time.' But inside, she felt a great surge of excitement. *This was it! It was happening!* She stood outside herself, seeing the way she was behaving, knowing she would remember it for the rest of her life. The ansaphone . . . No! She'd leave it off. Safer. Heart thumping, she ran downstairs, banged the front door shut, got into her car. Exultation sang through her. *He'd left her! He'd left her!* She tore past Roath Park Lake, swung the car right, belted down the other side in the opposite direction. *In the office! Waiting for her!* What had brought it about? She dared not think. It might only be a temporary thing. He could be back with her tomorrow. But to leave her like that, in the middle of the night! It must be serious! She shot across a red light, got a grip on herself. *Calm down, Eve, for God's sake. Or you'll end up being dead, and what good will that do?* She turned into Newport Road, then down the dual carriageway to Cardiff Bay. *There on his own. Waiting for her. Jesus!*

His car was there, parked outside: she wasn't dreaming. A screech of brakes, and she was out of the

193

car and clip-clopping along the tarmac. He opened the door for her. She clung to him. 'Oh Colin, my love, my love.' Kissing him. Standing there in the dark. He murmured her name. This was it. Amazing. Amazing.

Drinking coffee, God knows how long later. From the machine. Plastic cups. There, in the office. Both of them. At this unearthly hour. Taking it all in. Trying to.

'You told her? About me?' Not anger, but amazement. Because he'd left her. It was incredible.

'But why now? What started it?'

'I don't know,' he said miserably. 'It just –' He shook his head.

'Don't think about it. We'll talk later.' She was in control; had to be.

'But we can't stay here,' she cried later. 'What am I thinking of? Come back to my place.'

The sudden wonder in his eyes. Seeing she belonged to him. Completely.

Then switching on the alarm again, leaving the office, locking up, driving away. Two cars, one after the other. No incriminating evidence. They'd tidied up carefully. Back along Newport Road, taxis here and there, little else, then through the broad thoroughfare of Albany Road to Ninian Road and her flat. Key in the lock, up two flights of stairs and there they were. Alone.

Suddenly it all seemed so right, it could have been scripted. 'Sit down,' she said calmly. 'Relax. Would you like a drink? Scotch?'

'No. Coffee please.'

'Sure now?'

'Yes.'

'White?'

'Please. The usual.'

194

The usual. A tremor ran through her. He sat, pale and dazed. *Like a road accident victim,* she thought. A black coffee for herself. Calm now, she sat opposite.

'So what happened?'

'She thought you were Sharon.'

'*What?*'

'I know it's stupid. So stupid that –' He began laughing, leaning his cheek into his left hand.

'She thought I was *Sharon.* What do you mean?'

He was helpless. He put the mug down, wiping his eyes with his handkerchief. 'Oh dear,' he said, fighting to control the hysteria. 'I'm sorry . . . sorry.'

He blew his nose. 'I'm sorry about that, Eve.'

'That's OK,' she said calmly. 'But how could she mistake me for Sharon?'

'It was going to London. For the conference. She thought Sharon was with me.'

'You told her that?'

'*No.*'

'Then how –'

'I didn't tell her anything. I just said I was going. But she got it into her head that . . .'

'Why?'

'I don't know. One of those things.'

Yvonne pondered this in silence. 'You must have made her suspicious. Have you said anything about me?'

'No. I wouldn't do that, Eve.'

She stared, not quite believing him.

'I haven't said a word,' he said stoutly. 'I told you.'

'Men can't keep secrets,' she said. 'There's something about them.'

He knew what she meant; he had felt the guilt oozing out of him, seen the knowledge in Kate's eyes.

'But why tonight?' Yvonne persisted. 'What brought it on?'

'I don't know,' he said wonderingly. 'That's the point.' He thought back through the chaos of the last few hours, grappling with the unreality of it all. 'I went home and it was dark – there weren't any lights on. She was lying on the bed. I thought she was dead for a minute. I tell you I did,' he insisted, seeing Yvonne's expression. 'I really did. Then she started on me.'

'Why?'

'I don't know. She was raving. Then it all came out. *You and that woman,* she said.'

'That woman,' said Yvonne flatly.

'Yes. Sharon.'

'That's what she said – Sharon.'

'Yes.'

'And you hadn't said a thing.'

'No.'

'I don't understand. Why should she suddenly start talking about Sharon?'

'I told you – she was suspicious.'

'Yes but *then.* Why then? Don't you see? Where'd she been?'

'I don't know.'

'You don't know much do you, Colin?' she said sarcastically.

He flushed. 'I don't put tabs on her. How should I know what she's doing all day?'

'You're too trusting. She could be up to anything.'

Like me, he thought, but did not say it.

'Has it ever struck you,' Yvonne said coolly, 'that she could be having an affair?'

'Don't be silly.'

'What's silly about it? You are.'

'I'd know if she was.'

'Would you? How?'

'I don't know. I just would.'

'I doubt it. I think she's a very clever woman.'

'You've hardly met her.'

'I don't need to. I know.'

It was the sort of thing Kate might have said. He stayed silent.

'Well,' said Yvonne, with a little movement of the shoulders that suggested a shrugging off of everything. 'We can't stay up all night. We'd better get some shut-eye.'

The word 'shut-eye' reassured him, for no special reason.

'Would you like a bath? You can have one if you like. It might settle you.'

'I feel settled enough, thanks.' He smiled, stood up. 'Thanks for rescuing me. I really shouldn't have called you.'

'Of course you should. What are you thinking about? I'd have been cross if you didn't.'

She went to him, crossed her hands behind his neck. 'You don't have to stay if you don't want. I'll take you back there if you like. You can sleep in Charlie's office.'

'No thanks. I'll stay here, if you don't mind.'

'How pleasant of you.' She rubbed her nose against his.

There it was again, he thought. That unexpected use of the word 'pleasant.' So typical of her.

He held her to him. Absurdly, a voice inside him said *Sharon.*

21

'We start shooting in Week Six,' said Carol, giving her father a bleak look. She had woken early, after a ridiculous dream in which her last steady boyfriend, Guy Parry (not quite steady enough to be a partner), had rung up to ask her out to dinner. She could not remember if, in her dream, she had assumed that she would be paying, as usual.

'Marvellous!' said Ted.

'You look very happy today,' she said suspiciously. 'What's wrong?'

'That's not very nice, Carol.'

'It's not meant to be. Did you see that woman?'

'What woman?'

She sighed. 'Ffion whatsit, of course.'

'Oh. Her. Yes, I did.'

'Well?'

'Well what?'

'You're in one of those moods, are you. How did it go?'

'It went very well, thanks.'

'I hope you gave her some good quotes.'

'Yes, I did.'

'Well, let's hope she does something with it. I've just been up to see Arnold. He's getting a bit shirty.'

'About what?'

'You and me.'

'Oh. Maybe we shouldn't go on meeting like this.

I'm sorry,' he added quickly, seeing her look. 'But why? I mean, he was all right about it at first, wasn't he? Why the sudden change?'

'Rupert's been getting at him.'

'Oh.'

'Says he should have been told. As First Minister. All utter rubbish, of course.'

'You're joking! What's it got to do with him?'

Carol shrugged. 'The sort of stuff Jasper Taylor was raking up. Bad image of Wales. Nepotism. The Taffia.'

'Jesus Christ!' exploded Ted. 'This bloody country. It's impossible.'

'Don't speak too loud, Ted.' She pointed to where Elen Watkins would be sitting at her computer, listening to every word through the open door.

'But it's ridiculous, dragging all this up now. What's he want you to do, fire me?'

'Yes, that'd be a good idea, wouldn't it?' she said ironically. 'I hadn't thought of that.'

'I'm sorry,' Ted said, after a brief silence. 'I should never have taken this job. I should have known.'

'Week Six,' said Carol crisply. 'That's when we get the show on the road. You up for it?'

'Got to be, haven't I? Everything sorted with the cast?'

'Just about. Terri Durban's dropped out though.'

'Has she? Why?'

'Part not big enough.'

'Bloody hell. Who's she think she is?'

'You tell me.' She went to the door. 'Any chance of a coffee, Elen?' she asked sweetly. 'I need a shot of caffeine.'

'In a minute,' Elen said shortly. 'I'll just print this out first. Ted want one as well?'

'Please,' Ted called back.

'Right you are. We aren't entirely impossible, you know.'

Ted and Carol exchanged 'these bloody Welsh' looks. Carol sat at her desk again.

'So,' she said heavily. 'That woman.'

Ted's heart thumped. 'Ffion?'

'No. The other one. The one you thought might make a good character,' she added, as her father looked blank.

'Oh. You mean Kate.'

'If you say so. Well, will she?'

'Will she what?'

'Make a good character,' said Carol, her patience rapidly dissolving.

'She might,' said Ted dubiously. 'I haven't really thought about it.'

'Haven't you? You surprise me. I've been thinking. After Doug and Andrea separate. How about if he met someone else?'

'And?'

'That's up to you, isn't it? Can you come up with something?'

'I don't know. I might.'

'What the hell's wrong with you, Ted?' asked Carol sharply, flinging down the biro she'd been doodling with. 'You're in a world of your own today.'

'Maybe I am,' he said enigmatically.

'Well, snap out of it. We've got some serious thinking to do. We might be going on.'

'Going on?'

'A second series. Next autumn. This could be open-ended, did you know that?'

'Open ended? You mean . . .?'

'Yes. Network's interested. A soap from Wales. If this is good enough.'

'Good God.'

'Exactly. So stop pissing me about, Ted. Even though you seem to be half-way into Ffion's knickers.'

Sharon West and Matthew Slater weren't exactly an item, but they did enjoy having lunch with each other now and then. They had joined the Charles Lewis Partnership at roughly the same time, when the old guard were leaving and Sir Charles had decided to soldier on with a slimmed-down staff, the 'partnership' existing in name only with the retirement of his old pal, David Webb, once one of the brightest and best architects in Cardiff. Colin had been a newer recruit, Yvonne newer still. It was these two who were on Sharon's mind as she sat opposite Matthew in The Rhubarb Patch, one of the latest vegetarian restaurants in the Welsh capital.

'Well,' said Sharon contentedly. 'Interesting morning, wasn't it?'

Matthew, preoccupied with the delicate task of anointing his salad with mayonnaise, did not immediately answer.

'Mm? Interesting? Why?'

'Well,' responded Sharon, spearing a radish niftily and popping it into her mouth, 'Colin and Yvonne, of course.'

'What about them?'

'You're joking.'

Matthew, tonsured though not with deliberate monkish intent, looked at her vaguely.

'What do you mean?'

'Well, it sticks out a mile, doesn't it?'

'What does?'

Sharon sighed theatrically. 'You'll be the death of me, Matthew, honest to God.'

Matthew set the mayonnaise down firmly. 'Will you please tell me what the hell you're talking about?'

'Well, they're having an affair, aren't they?'

'Colin and Yvonne?'

'Of course.

'How do you know?'

'It sticks out a mile.'

'I hadn't noticed.'

'You're really sweet, Matthew. You know that?'

Matthew ignored this. 'I know she's dead set on him, that's obvious. But I can't imagine Colin . . .'

'Why not?'

'Well . . .' He shrugged. 'He's too straight.' Sharon made a derisory exclamation. 'Well? Isn't he?'

'He's a man.'

'Oh God,' said Matthew wearily. 'If you're going to give us all that . . .'

'Look. I'm not getting at you. But you know what I mean.'

'I'm sorry, but I don't. And I don't want to hear this. Really.'

'All right then. But it affects you.'

Matthew, not looking at her, wishing he had skipped lunch, munched away.

She ate her nut roast.

'How does it affect me?' he asked resentfully.

'Because Charlie's getting out soon. And he's going to offer us all a buy-out.'

Matthew, a portion of veggie lasagne half-way to his mouth, stared at her.

'How do you know that?'

'A little bird told me.'

'You're not serious?'

'As a judge.'

He put down his knife and fork. 'Come on,' he said. 'Give.'

Sharon, her face suffused a deeper pink than usual with self-satisfaction, gave. 'I saw Charlie's wife one day. In town. We had coffee together. She's quite matey, you know, once you get to know her.'

'I didn't know you did.'

'Well, only slightly. Christmas parties and things – you know.'

'All girls together – that it?' he asked ironically.

'Something like.'

'So what did she say?'

Sharon told him.

'Good God,' said Matthew at last. 'You're quite sure about this?'

'As sure as I can be about anything.'

'Maybe she's having you on.'

'Why should she be? She's got nothing to gain by it. But for God's sake don't let on I told you. She swore me to secrecy.'

'So I gather,' he said dryly.

'Only because of this Colin and Yvonne thing,' she said defensively. 'It might screw things up, mightn't it?'

'How?'

'Well, if Colin screws up his marriage who knows what might happen?'

'Mm . . . Nasty.'

'On the other hand . . .'

'Yes?'

'Yvonne's got money, hasn't she?'

'Has she?'

'You know who her father is, don't you?'

'No, I don't.'

She enlightened him.

'I see,' said Matthew reflectively. 'Mr Big, eh?'

'Something like.'

She was fond of the expression; this time he tried not to be irritated.

'So he might cough up?'

'He might. If he thought it would enhance his daughter's chances.'

'Of having Colin?'

'Of having anything.'

Matthew took all this in, a gleam enlivening his normally cold eye.

'Pity,' he said at last. 'I'm quite fond of Colin's wife.'

Jill Gosport was on the warpath. She had an up-and-downer with Pam over the mess left in the back room by a do-gooder who had muddily trailed in with a bright smile and green wellies, found fault over the way the men's used suits had been hung, and barely sympathised with Kate over the headache that had allegedly kept her away from work all morning. The pain in the chest, where Colin had thumped her, had almost gone.

'Bitch,' mouthed Pam when Jill slipped out and at last they had a moment together. 'Terry must be limper than usual. She ought to put some Viagra in his soup.'

Kate could not manage even the faintest of smiles.

'What's up then, dalling? Not just a headache, was it?' said Pam shrewdly.

'No,' Kate admitted.

'Dalling! What is it? Here.'

Kate dabbed her eyes with Pam's hankie. 'I can't, Pam. Sorry –'

'Go home,' Pam commanded. 'This minute. Go on. I'll cover for you.'

'I can't –'

'Yes you can. Quick, before she gets back. I'll come and see you later, when I finish.'

Kate fled, back to the empty house. She had been awake all night, expecting him to come back. The name Yvonne had swirled around in her head, the misty shape of the girl she hardly knew. At last she had dropped into a troubled sleep, and when she woke it was half-past eleven and her head was clear.

So she hadn't been imagining things. Colin *had* been lying about working late. He *had* been up to something in London. Only with Yvonne, not Sharon. What a fool she'd been! But how could she possibly have known?

She could not believe she was taking this so calmly. She looked at herself in the mirror. Who was she, this Kate Dawson? No, she corrected. Kate Mallin. She'd go back to her maiden name.

She had rung Jill at the charity shop to apologise for not turning up and to say she'd be in that afternoon. And now, home again, she fussed around with her indoor plants and waited for Pam.

'But what are you going to do?' asked Pam, intrigued, after Kate had gone over it all. 'Have it out with them?'

'No. I'm not going to do anything.'

'You're just going to let him go?'

'He's gone. That's it. I don't want him back.'

'But it's all happened so quickly! I can't believe –'
She stared at Kate, eyes popping.

Kate felt a surge of triumph. She was important! She could cope! Yet at the same time she knew it was not that easy; there'd be a price to pay. She was the numbed victim of disaster; when feeling returned, she would suffer.

'What if he comes back – tonight?' Pam's eyes shone with the excitement of it all; she too had a part to play in Kate's drama.

'He won't.'

'But if he did, dalling – what would you do?'

'Kill him, probably.'

'Oh dalling!' Pam all but clapped her hands.

When Pam left at last, Kate switched on the telly. She waited for something to happen; the phone to ring; Colin's car to come up the drive.

All she heard were the voices on telly. Inane voices, speaking of nothing. She sat there, absorbing the voices to fill the emptiness inside.

22

In his lighter moments Gwynne Tecwyn would say that while he could live without women, he couldn't live without Cardiff City. He had been a fan ever since moving down to the Welsh capital from Bala to be where the action was, as he liked to put it. He'd been far more successful as a scriptwriter than City had as a football club, steadily winning commissions from the Welsh television channel, S4C, while City continued to languish in the lower divisions of the Football League. His record with Cambrian TV and the BBC had been more iffy, and he still felt outraged by the way Carol Hart had dumped him in favour of her father. He had now been dumped a second time, by Ffion Tomos, a peculiarly hurtful blow to his pride. Saturday afternoons at Ninian Park provided solace of a kind, especially as the team had begun to win a few matches. It had been even better when Nathan Blake was still in the team, a strong young striker who had the extra merit, for Gwynne Tecwyn, of being black. As a Welsh-speaking Welshman in Wales's mainly monoglot capital, he empathised with minorities. 'Come on, Blakey!' he'd yell from the popular bank, where he found no difficulty at all in reconciling his loathing of racism with the shouting of scurrilous abuse of the English. Blakey, of course, hadn't been with City long. He'd gone up and away to a higher division, maintaining the club's consistent policy of selling all its best players.

Gwynne consoled himself with the hope that maybe, come the Millennium, things would get better. What the club needed was a Saviour, someone who would take it by the scruff of the neck and make it undoubtedly the best in Wales.

Scuffling along Sloper Road after an unmemorable match, Gwynne's eye was caught by a discarded page from that day's *Cardiff Voice*, flapping around some iron railings. The name 'Ffion Tomos' blazed out like a trumpet call in an empty theatre. He bent and picked up the page, causing a supporter close behind to bump into him and snarl something not too flattering. He stuffed the page into his pocket and strode briskly on. 'Ffion Tomos, Ffion Tomos' repeated a taunting voice in his head. As the crowd thinned out he had space enough to take the page from his pocket but was reluctant to do so. He was scared of that name, 'Ffion Tomos', in case it might damage him. It wasn't until he was back in his terraced house in Canton that he dredged up the courage to read her feature on Ted Sloane. 'Christ,' he muttered, when he came to the end of it. 'The bitch. The utter bitch.' It seemed a betrayal far worse than the petulant way she had finished with him, for it was directed at the very heart of his idea of himself as a successful, creative person. How could she bring herself to boost his most hated rival like this? Every word scalded him.

He tore the page into shreds before stuffing it into the plastic bag of rubbish in his kitchen. He sat down, holding his head in his hands.

'Well,' said Carol, 'you happy with that?'

She had gone along to his cottage on that Saturday afternoon, with a copy of the *Cardiff Voice* which she knew he would not have gone out to buy for himself.

'Yes,' Ted replied coolly. 'It's OK, isn't it?'

'OK? It's bloody marvellous. How'd she get those quotes out of you? Or did she make them all up?'

'No, they're all right – more or less.'

Sitting with her back to the window that overlooked the river bridge, she looked at him shrewdly. There was something different about him, a slackening of the tension at the corners of his mouth, an air of self-satisfaction.

'You must have got on pretty well with her,' said Carol dryly.

'Yes. I suppose I did.'

She weighed a remark in the balance and felt the scales tip down to one side.

'How well?'

'Well enough,' he replied with a smile.

'Having an affair with her, are you?'

'Don't be so damned personal.'

'You know,' said Carol, after a long silence. 'I used to hate you at one time. The way you left Mum for Letty – and then married her . . .'

'I know,' said Ted quietly.

'Then when I came to know Letty . . . It wasn't easy, you know,' she cried.

'I never imagined it was . . . I'm sorry, love.'

'Bloody life. That's what it is.'

Hasn't worked out too well for you, has it? thought Ted, thinking of her string of broken romances. He said nothing.

'Well,' Carol said, 'good luck to you. But watch your step. I hear she's a man-eater.'

'H'm. Don't suppose I'll taste very good.'

Yvonne knew it wouldn't be easy; Colin wasn't the sort to go easily from one woman to another. That first night, after she had rescued him from the office, he slept on the settee while she lay alone in her double bed, at once thrilled and apprehensive.

The second night, their cars drawn up next to each other outside after their return from the office, he was like someone in shock. He ate little; spoke little; looked at her with dazed, uncomprehending eyes.

She waited for the phone to ring, for Kate to turn up at her door, demanding her man back. Nothing happened.

They sat side by side, holding hands, watching – or rather, not watching – the telly. They had a late-night coffee and then she said neutrally, 'Coming to bed then?'

'I don't know,' he said. 'I really don't know.'

'She won't be coming now. It's too late.'

'I knew she wouldn't. She told me.' Yvonne looked at him. 'When I rang.'

'Of course,' said Yvonne quietly. 'Well,' she added after a moment, 'I'm turning in. You can come if you like. Or stay here if you want. It's up to you.'

'You don't mind me staying?'

'Mind?' she said, smiling. 'Why should I mind?'

He shrugged, looking lost. She turned at the door and said, 'You can go back to her if you like, you know. It's entirely up to you.'

'I can't do that.'

'Because she won't have you?'

'Because I don't want to.'

They looked at each other. 'Well,' she said.

They went into the bedroom together and kissed.

'You're sure now?' she murmured.

He nodded.

Waking in the night, she heard a strange sound, then realised it was Colin crying. She put her arm around him, stroked his head. 'It's all right, darling,' she whispered.

'I know. It's just that –'

'Don't. Don't say anything.'

When at last he slept again, she lay awake, wondering.

She heard his car come up the drive a dozen times a day in her head, his key turn in the lock. She saw him walk into the room where she was sitting, staring at nothing, his head bowed in penitence, his blue eyes dark with remorse. 'I'm sorry, darling,' he said. 'I've been so stupid. Can you forgive me?'

She realised he had been gone only two full days, that the postman would call any moment with still more letters for him to add to those already stacked on the small table in the hall. She wondered how he was managing without his shirts and socks and pants – he changed them every day, naturally – and realised he must have gone out shopping for new clothes, new ties, even, because he never wore the same one two days running. It was the thought of him buying new ties that got to her most, for some reason: there was an element of pathos in it.

Waking early, she wept, seeing the whole day in front of her without him, day following day, month following month. She wanted him back so that they could go on with the sheer ordinariness of life, she getting annoyed with the put-putting of his lips on the pipe – what other man his age smoked a pipe, for God's sake – while he pretended not to notice that, inside, she was boiling over. They had gone on so long like this, when had it started to alter? And how had it come to this nightmare, his leaving in the dead of night after she had attacked him?

Suspicion, suspicion, it was all down to suspicion! That's when the poison had set in, to trickle its deadliness into the bloodstream of their marriage. His constant working late at the office, the subtle change she felt in him, Joyce's hints dropped slyly into their coffee-time conversations, then the weekend in London and her own reckless reaction to this, that brush-off by Ted Sloane that had sent her skittering home with her tail between her legs, and that moment – how dreadful – when she had accused him wildly over Sharon, knowing he would deny it, that the affair had existed only in her mind! But instead of reassurance, out the truth had come – Yvonne!

She could not bear to think of them together. She could not picture it even; it was so bizarre. She did not know the girl; had seen her only a few times, when dropping into the office; and once, at some social function she could not properly remember. Yvonne – silly French name! – had made no impression on her in the least. How long had Colin been in love with her? *Was* he in love, or just infatuated with her? Where did infatuation end, and love begin? Her head whirled with the impossibility of it all.

She would have to go out; she couldn't stay in the house alone. But where could she go? She had been so enclosed within herself these past few years that she had few friends; her life had revolved around Colin and his work. Now she had Pam but she did not know her home number, and anyway she wouldn't bother her today. She could not walk along the lane for fear of meeting Ted; next door Joyce would be hard pressed coping with the kids.

She felt the size and weight of the house around her. It was too big, far too big. And it was filled now with the emptiness of Colin's absence.

She sat down, exhausted. The phone rang. It was Colin, asking if he might call round the next morning.

23

She had meant to be calm, to talk it over rationally, but directly she saw him in that absurd new gear of his, something snapped. That trendy leather jacket, those cavalry twill trousers! Who did he think he was?

'Where did you get that new outfit, Colin?' she mocked. 'You look like something out of a mail order catalogue.'

'Thank you very much,' he said coldly.

'Did she buy it for you? I can't say I admire her taste.'

'As a matter of fact I bought it myself. Do you mind if I sit down?'

'Feel free. It's your house, in case you've forgotten.'

He sat on the settee by the window, looking so out of place in those ridiculous clothes that it was as if she had never seen him sitting there before in her life. She had wondered how she would face him, but the change in his outward appearance made it easy. Absurdly, she wanted to laugh.

'Would you like some coffee?' she asked. 'We might as well be civilised about this.'

'If you like.'

'Do you take milk and sugar? I can't remember.'

He gave her a look. She smiled sweetly, and went to the kitchen.

It was while pouring the coffee from the percolator that she found her hand suddenly shaking. She had to put the percolator down, fight back the tears that came so unexpectedly.

How could he do this? What had happened to them?

'I don't know what you want from me, Colin,' she said, back in the living-room. 'But I don't think I want to talk to you much today, really.'

'I'm sorry, Kate,' he said humbly. 'I'm truly sorry.'

'Sorry!' she cried. 'Sorry for what?'

'Everything.'

'I think you're sorry for yourself. You always have been. Sorry you married someone like me.'

'Now, Kate –'

'Don't Kate me! It's true and you know it. We've been a disaster. A complete and utter disaster.'

He wanted to deny it but simply sat there, suffering. Part of him reached out to her, for hadn't she always been like this? Self-pity mixed with self-disgust in her nature, poison and pathos intermingled.

'Why didn't you tell me?' she asked, with sudden spirit. 'I had no idea this *Yvonne* . . .' She faltered, unable to complete the sentence.

'There was nothing to tell, Kate. It's just happened.'

'Oh, is that so? A fling then, is it? Is that what you're saying? Because if so –'

'No! I'm not saying that at all!'

'What are you saying then?'

He shrugged, determined not to weaken.

'I don't understand you,' she said wearily. 'You always seemed so bloody perfect.'

'I never said I was. That's you talking, not me.'

'And that pipe of yours! God.'

He stared at her, surprised anew at her capacity for irrelevance.

'You know,' she mused, 'I hated you for it. Funny, isn't it?'

'Hated me for what?'

'Your utter devotion. You got on my nerves. Just sitting there, taking it. Serves me right, doesn't it?'

'I don't know what you're talking about,' he lied.

She saw that he was still what he always had been: complacent, self-absorbed, wearing an invisible shield against obscure hurts which she would never fathom.

'I only hope she knows what she's letting herself in for,' she said.

He looked at her uncomfortably, and she knew that, for once, she had drawn the faintest trickle of blood.

'There's no coming back, you know, Colin,' she said. 'You've made your bed and you must lie on it.'

He smiled faintly, amused by the cliché.

After he had left, she wrapped herself in the stillness of the house. She was surprised by how calm she felt. His visit, although brief, had forced her to take the step she had been avoiding, the first step away from her old life towards the new. What the new life would be she did not know, except that it would not be lived in Cardiff. Neither would it be in Ireland; there was no going back there. She felt a stirring inside her, a lifting of her spirits. She was still young; she was healthy; she had faith in herself. Wonderingly, she realised how much she had changed these past few weeks. Working in the charity shop had given her confidence; she had proved she could cope. No more the little stay-at-home, scared to face the big bad world! And then there was Ted. She thought of him now with amusement. How she had idolised him! But now? She admired him still, but now it was an admiration fatally mixed with pity. To see a once-famous author brought low was not a pretty sight. She had left his cottage that day feeling hurt and angry but now, from her altered position, she was able to view him indulgently. He had been good to her; good *for* her. Going to the party with him had boosted her morale. And she'd have his book to remember him by, the signed copy of *Eden's Rock* she would forever treasure.

She took it from the shelf, flipped through the pages. It was a fine novel; yet dated. And she knew he would never write another.

Pleased by this objectivity, she sat down, the book in her hand. She felt she was beginning a journey.

'That it?'

'No. A bit more to the left . . . That's too far . . . A teeny bit more . . . That's it. Perfect.'

Ffion smiled up at him. Ted looked quizzically down from the chair he was standing on to put up the Christmas decorations in his cottage.

'You sure now?'

'Positive. Absolutely.'

Happiness gave Ffion's voice a new fullness, her eyes a brightness that would have surprised those who saw her only as a chilly operator in the cut-throat world of communications.

'You can come down now, Ted.'

'Thank you.'

He smiled down at her. He too was changed, his whole being more relaxed and open.

'You know, I never thought you would,' she admitted.

'Would what?'

'Put up trimmings like this. Get all Christmassy.'

'Why not? You think I'm past it?'

'No, no – not past it. Just –'

He looked at her.

'Well.' She didn't find this easy. 'To be quite honest, I thought you'd be too disillusioned by it all.'

'Disillusioned,' he repeated, deadpan.

'Don't get me wrong, Ted. I mean – I didn't know you. But there were rumours – that you were difficult.'

'Difficult? Me?' He feigned disbelief.

'Come on now, darling. You know what I mean. You had a reputation – for not giving interviews. That sort of thing.'

'Did I? Can't understand why.'

'And now look at you. You'll talk to anyone. *The Guardian, The Independent, The Observer . . .*'

'Even the *Torygraph,*' he agreed. 'Who'd have thought it?

'Exactly.'

'And you know who started it all, don't you?' He put his arm around her shoulders.

'Yes. Conrad Matthews.'

'Good old Conrad.' He kissed her lightly; then less lightly.

The 'For Sale' sign went up on the house late in February. True to form, Joyce was the first to spot it.

'Wonder where she's going?' asked Derek. 'Back to Ireland, do you think?'

'God knows,' said Joyce bitterly. 'She doesn't tell me a thing. Didn't even know the house was going up for sale. There's friendship for you.'

Derek glanced at her curiously. He wondered why his wife felt so strongly about it. A thoughtful man, he reflected on the mystery of marriage: you were always finding out something new about your partner, even if that were someone as obviously transparent (or so she appeared to be) as Joyce.

She then said something which reminded him of her utter predictability in some matters.

'Wish *I* was going. I'm sick of Cardiff.'

With difficulty, he suppressed a sigh.

'I'm not staying here till the day I die, that's for sure,' she added feelingly.

'I'm not asking you to, pet.' He snapped off the telly with the remote; they weren't really looking at it anyway.

'What's that supposed to mean?' She felt outraged by the endearment, 'pet'; he must know how she hated it. Was he annoying her deliberately? 'Your practice is here, isn't it? The kids are in school. There's no hope for me.'

'God, Joyce, you're so dramatic!' He was amused but tried not to show it. 'Anyone'd think you were serving a life sentence.'

'I am. I bloody am. A life sentence in Cardiff.'

No need to ask where she wanted to go; he knew the script off by heart. *There's no sea here . . . You call Penarth the sea? . . .Piddling little waves that wouldn't knock a cat over . . . I miss the prom and Pen Dinas . . . the town . . .'*

Aber-bloody-ystwyth. He wished the Normans had stayed away instead of building one of their stupid castles there. The place wouldn't have existed then, rat hole that it was. He could no more live in Aberystwyth than do a ton in a fog along the M4. But he couldn't tell Joyce that. He had to humour her.

'Look, love,' he said reasonably. 'I won't be working all my life. I'll retire early if I can. We can talk about living in Aber then.'

'I'll be dead and buried by then. You can go to the south of France with your fancy woman.'

Fancy woman! Some hopes. She knew how straight he was, or she wouldn't have said it.

Mind, sometimes he thought it wasn't such a bad idea. He found himself wishing Kate had applied for that job as his receptionist.

Suvla commanded a fine view of Swansea Bay. George and Thelma Morris, having only a shaky grasp of modern history and no knowledge at all of the Gallipoli campaign in the Great War, had no idea why their house was so named, but they were quite certain that it suited them down to the ground. They had lived there now for fifteen years, and seen their children, Yvonne and Russell, safely through adolescence in this eminently desirable location on the edge of Mumbles.

They were quite certain too that they thoroughly approved of Colin Dawson, the go-ahead architect their daughter had taken up with in a big way these last few months. They had been wary at first, naturally worried at the fact that he was a married man. But the obvious break-up of the marriage, and Yvonne's frequent deunciations of his bitch of a wife, had helped them adjust to the reality of the situation, realising that they really had no choice: either they had Yvonne and Colin, or they didn't have Yvonne at all.

The more George saw of Colin, the better he liked him. He seemed a straight sort of chap, amiable to a degree, and for the life of him he couldn't see why any woman wouldn't do her damnedest to hold on to him. Moreover he was a man with prospects, and as a successful businessman George liked people with prospects. His interest became keener when he discovered that Colin's boss was retiring and putting his architect's practice in Cardiff Bay up for sale. He was evidently open to the idea of a buy-out by his staff, so long as they had the wherewithal. The wherewithal was somewhat lacking at the moment, but he had the means to come up with it if he wanted to. But he wouldn't rush into it – oh no. It all depended how things panned out with Colin and Yvonne. He'd give them a while longer . . .

Colin was settling down with Yvonne far better than he'd expected. He was getting used to her now, her body and her ways. She was far less prickly than Kate; more naïve, more innocent; she deferred to him in situations in which Kate would have challenged him; yet intolerant of things which Kate had tolerated (or only just tolerated), such as his pipe. 'I can't *stand* the stink of that!' Yvonne cried. 'And the mess! Why do you need it, Colin? Only old men smoke pipes.' He had missed it at first, the feel of the tobacco as he pressed it into the bowl – he could tell which brand it was, just from touch – the slow ceremony of lighting up, the languorous way the dark blue smoke drifted across the room . . . There was something almost sensual about it . . . But he had let it all go, and already it had become something posthumous, part of the old, dead life he had buried for good.

What Colin loved most about Yvonne was that she was a *friend*. Their sex life was OK, but nothing special. Where Yvonne scored was in the fact that she actually seemed to like him. She was nice to him; valued what he did for her; enjoyed all the little things that, in his marriage, had been swamped by Kate's perpetual edginess, the darkness in her soul.

Yet he was not altogether free of Kate. How could he be? Her soft Irish voice spoke to him in the dead of night, saying nothing distinctive but murmuring, murmuring. He would wake up, his head boiling with guilt and remorse. He had meant his marriage to last; how could it have been destroyed so quickly ?

He knew the answer: because it had been built on quicksands that had finally sucked it down into nothingness. Colin and Kate, Kate and Colin; the ghosts of their former selves fretted in the deep-down darkness, forever picking at each other, forever discontent.

Punters got off to a flying start, with upbeat reviews in the *Western Mail* and *Daily Post*. Ratings were good from the word go, and they soared spectacularly as the series progressed. After a while even the BBC couldn't ignore Ted Sloane, although he was working for the opposition. He was interviewed by Roy Noble, appeared as a pundit in studio discussions, and when the drama department in Cardiff commissioned a play from him he seemed to be on Radio Wales every other week.

'Happy now then, are you?' asked Carol over a pub lunch one day.

'Happy enough,' Ted conceded.

'You ought to be. Good ratings, a new woman in your life . . . what else do you want?'

'I don't know.' And then he saw her again, the woman standing on the bridge by his cottage, staring down at the water. He had a sudden sense of irretrievable loss. Those kisses at the Hallowe'en party might have led somewhere. What a fool he'd been!

'I wonder what happened to her?' he murmured.

'Who?'

He was at a loss for a moment, not realising he had spoken aloud. 'The woman I used to see walking in the lane. Kate something.'

Carol stared at her father, amused. 'What made you think of her?'

'I really don't know.'

'She called on you once, didn't she? You took her to the canteen.'

'Yes, I did.'

'Did you take her anywhere else?' Carol asked mischievously.

'I didn't take her to bed, if that's what you're thinking.'

Carol pretended to look shocked. 'The very idea.' She looked thoughtful. 'You were going to put her into *Punters,* weren't you? A new character.'

'I did think of it, yes. But we didn't need her in the end, did we?'

'No. Just as well. We'd have gone over budget.'

Ted shook his head, as if ridding himself of a bad old idea. 'I didn't know what to make of her anyway. She mystified me.'

'Did Ffion ever meet her?' asked Carol curiously.

'No. Yes,' he corrected. 'Once.'

Carol was about to say something, but changed her mind. She looked at her father fondly. The time she had been alienated from him seemed so distant now. He was an old rogue, but a nice one.

'Nice to see you looking so happy, Dad.'

'I am,' Ted replied.

Kate was reading a lot, not only her set books but others she'd never tried before. Proust she detested, but she'd discovered an unexpected liking for Zola.

She had struck lucky with Griff, a large and seemingly careless man who exerted an odd spell over his students. They seemed to worship him, but she didn't. She was, however, indulgent of him, and he of her. It was a relaxed, almost offhand relationship.

'You're not working *today*, are you?' he asked drowsily, waking just in time to see her set off.

'I told you I was. You don't listen, that's your trouble.'

'But bank holidays, God . . . doesn't that place ever close?'

'Not on bank holidays it doesn't. We'll be knee-deep in tourists.'

'Sod the tourists. We could be going out somewhere.'

'Where, for instance?'

His lips squeezed out into an ironical pout. 'I don't know. The Planetarium? The Tower?'

'Oh, charming. That'd be a real busman's holiday for me, wouldn't it?'

'Thought you'd enjoy that. Seeing you love the tourists so much.'

'Not that much, sunshine. Go back to sleep.' She bent to kiss him briefly through his hedgehog-prickly beard. 'See you later. 'Bye.'

He answered with a grunt, and heard her – just – close the front door before he slipped back into sleep. He snored, gently and rhythmically. The late August sun, surprised by a gap in the clouds, tentatively illumined the spines of a row of books that Kate took with her everywhere.